s h r i n k a g e

a ^{little} novel: that grows on you...

luke young

NPP

PUBLISHED BY NEW PERENNIAL PRESS

ISBN: 978-0-692-01203-1

Cover photo credits: Hemera/Thinkstock and IStockphoto/Thinkstock

TO MY WIFE,

Lucky for her, only a small part of this novel is loosely based on the truth. No, not that part. I'm serious...

contents

shrinkage

prologue - I thought you were talking about a blowjob or something!

They say people never change, but Tim Garrett was different now. He had changed tremendously in the last couple of weeks and he was really enjoying his new life. His once floundering sex life was now flourishing, he was in better shape, and his thinning hair was actually growing back. The girl whose bed he was now lying in would not have given him a second look before, because before he wasn't her type at all. But now he was exactly what she was looking for and he was in her bed, a place he had fantasized about, but never thought he would ever be. The only problem was that in his fantasy, he was never face down, naked, spread eagle and strapped to the bed like an animal. The straps came up from each corner of the bed and were attached to his arms and legs. They were super strong; Tim wasn't going anywhere.

He probably would have agreed to pretty much anything she had asked, but she really didn't ask to restrain him. It just kind of happened. Tim definitely hadn't known that this was what she had in mind; if he had, he never would have gone to her apartment in the first place.

His captor certainly looked incredible in her matching bright yellow lace bra and panties as she stood over him, studying the case full of assorted dildos. Tim wasn't sure exactly what she was doing, but it seemed that she was trying to select the one most closely matched to his size as he lay there with his face smashed into the sheets, barely able to move.

While she was distracted by this important decision, Tim quietly tested the strength of the restraints, found them quite strong, and then lifted his head off the mattress to see what had her so preoccupied. After catching a brief glimpse of the case's contents, he yanked the straps hard and when they didn't budge, he whined, "I really don't want to do this."

She said in a mockingly sweet voice, "But you said I could do anything."

"I thought you were talking about a blowjob or something!" He struggled to get a better look in the case and when he did he said, "You, uh, got some really big ones."

She tossed the largest one down in front of his face and it landed with a loud thump. He eyed it, horrified, as she said, "None do you justice, but this is the closest. I call him Kong."

Tim pleaded, "Funny story. Two weeks ago I was actually really, uh, small. I took this enlargement pill. Just call my ex-girlfriend Jill Taylor. Seriously."

Tim was actually telling the truth. Just two weeks prior to this, he had been smaller in the penis department; a lot smaller. He was also not lying about it being a funny story either. Let's start at the beginning...

one - What the fuck could Actor/Director/Oil spill cleanup expert Kevin Costner possibly have to do with any of this? I mean seriously!

Is it in yet? It's the phrase that no man ever wants to hear. I'm sure any guy would take, *Get out of your car now or I'm going to kill you,* or even, *You only have six months to live,* over those other five words any day. Okay, maybe not the six months to live thing, but you get the point. Luckily, Tim had never heard those words. At least he had never heard them out loud.

Tim was twenty-six and sure he had packed on a few pounds since college, but you wouldn't call him fat; maybe just a little out of shape for someone his age. Life had not been very kind to him and clear evidence of that was his thinning hair. The early onset baldness was bizarre and especially cruel given that Tim had been denied a normal adolescence and hit puberty ungodly late.

You would think a guy burdened with the absolute fucking nightmare of not hitting puberty full on until the second half of his freshman year at college would be spared hair loss altogether. Or if there were an ounce of justice in this world, he'd at least have a full head of hair well into his fifties. Unfortunately, that was not the case for Tim. The hair started falling out early, and it was not a good look for him. But his real problem was, well… the problem was his penis, his slightly to possibly mildly below average penis. Despite all these issues, he did actually have a girlfriend and it was his longest relationship to date. Nearly nine months.

It was Saturday afternoon and Tim was on his way to the drug store. It was going to be a big night for him and his girlfriend, Jill. He'd been planning it for a week. He would prepare her favorite meal of fresh steamed lobster served with a side of blue cheese pecan chopped salad. This would be the third time he was making lobster for her, and since times one and two resulted in amazing sex, he was thoroughly confident that this time would be no different.

Tim picked up everything he needed for the perfect evening, including a special bottle of wine and her favorite peach carnations. He even went to the farmers market to buy fresh vegetables for the salad. All that he needed now was to restock his condom supply, a task that filled Tim with dread.

As Tim drove past the billboard of the male underwear model busting out of his boxer briefs, he scoffed. He'd driven past it dozens of times on his way to the drug superstore, and it wasn't the only reminder of his little problem; the reminders were all around him. From super-sized ad campaigns to phallic inspired architecture to penis jokes on television and in movies to country songs titled "Size Matters," it was difficult to believe anything other than size really did matter.

The billboard reminded him of that Kevin Costner baseball movie, no not *Bull Durham* or *Field of Dreams*; the other one, the one that flopped at the box office. Kevin's full frontal nude scene in *For Love of the Game* was reportedly deleted after test screenings, where the audience openly laughed at Kevin's manhood. They actually openly laughed, as if everyone in the audience was hung like a freaking horse, or was sleeping with someone who was hung like a freaking horse. Tim wondered if it really needed to hang to your knees in order to not garner a snicker? And at what size does that snicker transform into jaw-dropping male locker-room jealousy and female awe?

Tim hated the fact that if he looked in the back of pretty much any magazine, he found ads for male enhancement products. Even in some women's magazines. As if anyone needs the girlfriend or wife saying, "Hey honey, you know that little penis you have? Well there's this pill..."

The worst was the spam email. Tim's company had this spam blocking software that collected all the suspicious messages he received and packaged them up into a single email, which listed all the obscene subject lines. The message normally contained hundreds of listings, and was delivered every Monday morning, providing a comical way to kick off an otherwise boring day. Subjects like: *Make Her Shiver With Your Girth*, *Longer Harder Thicker Naturally Guaranteed*, *Gain 3 Inches Now*, *Power Pack That Tool In Your Pants*, and Tim's personal favorite: *Face It, She's Dreaming Of Something Bigger And We Can Help*. They can help you all right; help separate you from your money. Oh, but you could always take advantage of the money back guarantee - just call customer service and explain how your penis is still really tiny and ask for a refund. Yeah right. It was a huge business, with huge promises but absolutely no results. Tim wondered how they got away with it.

He'd done his research. He was just slightly below average in length at 5.53 inches. Not 5.5, that would be selling him short, but exactly 5.53 inches. And he really didn't have any issue with the length. Hell, most of the nerve endings were in the outer third of the uh, well you know, the woman's private parts. At least this was what he kept telling himself, since he was almost sure he remembered reading it somewhere.

The real problem was the girth. At 3.95 inches around, it was slim by any standard all right - a real pencil dick. By comparing various surveys, Tim found that 4.75 inches was the average girth and even that didn't really do the trick if you thought about it. As everyone knew, the female vagina could open itself up wide enough to deliver an entire baby, which is a pretty incredible and frightening thing. Now that's not to say you need to be packing a penis the size of a baby's head, but there's a lot of discrepancy between what the average guy has and what is required to actually fill that thing up. Would the world stop spinning, Tim thought, if he were just a little bigger?

Tim often wondered how different his life would have been if he were huge down there. He'd imagined what some of his past relationships would have been like if there hadn't been what he perceived as a disappointment to the girl he was dating when it finally came to having sex. Was he imagining it? He didn't think so. He wondered how much more confident he would have been if, when he dropped his pants, he could see mouthwatering awe and desire in their eyes. He pictured what a look of, *Okay big boy be careful with that thing* was like as opposed to the *Really, is that it?* look that he was almost sure he had seen in the past.

But those days were over for Tim when he lucked out and found a girl who didn't seem to be so caught up on size. His girlfriend Jill had a smoking hot little body. She was a bit of a mystery in that when they had sex, he felt something was just a little off, just a tiny little bit, but she did always seemed to be right there with him. She didn't seem to be fantasizing of something more. Most of the time, anyway. There were only a few moments here and there when he wasn't sure.

When they acquired their first sex toy together, it wasn't ridiculously huge or anything. It was certainly bigger than he was, but not terribly threatening. Later he discovered that Jill had a separate secret dildo collection and each one seemed to be bigger than the next. He wasn't sure if she purchased these big boys before or after they started dating, and he wasn't sure if he really cared. Anyway, they were about to move in together and it felt right. He was happy; he was almost ninety percent sure. Okay, maybe eighty-five percent.

two - Your secret's safe with me

Tim pulled into the drugstore parking lot. This store happened to be the only one he knew that stocked his special brand. He always preferred to buy online to avoid the embarrassment, but it was an emergency so he would have to tough it out and deal with the potential humiliation.

When Tim reached the condom aisle, he realized it was, of course, the same aisle that housed the feminine hygiene products, just as it was in most of the stores he'd been in. He wondered whose idea this was? The last thing he needed while scrutinizing the condoms was to find a group of women pondering what type of pad they might like to try. Invariably, whenever he was forced to buy condoms in a store, he would find the aisle crawling with women and this day was no different.

When he rounded the corner, he found two women in the aisle and he paused at the end cap display, pretending to browse the items there. When it appeared the ladies were there for the long haul, he sighed, left the aisle, picked up some shaving cream, toothpaste, and other toiletries he didn't need, and then returned. When he found it occupied still, he took a deep breath. He had waited long enough and he had a great night of sex ahead of him. His plan was to head down the aisle past the women, quickly scan the shelf, pick out his box and dump them into his basket.

His plan went awry when he approached the area where his special condoms should have been stocked and they were not there. He began a frantic search, scanning the shelves and pushing boxes out of the way in order to see what was behind them. The store seemed to have every other kind of condom available - colored, textured, lubricated, un-lubricated, even ones with spiky things shooting out of them (what the hell do those actually do?), and they also had a shit load of boxes of those *look at me, my dick is so big that a regular little boy condom just won't contain my hugeness* super-sized ones. They had two whole sections of them. Aren't only like less than five percent of guys supposed to "need" those? It was as if the store expected a whole pro basketball team to be pulling up in a bus at any moment.

He was starting to make quite a mess of the section with his ransacking and was about to give up when he moved aside one last box and found the holy grail of condoms as far as he was concerned - the oddly-named Mini XS Ultra Snug Fit condoms. The Mini XS's were just a little more snug-fitting than your standard condoms. It was nothing to laugh at. Some guys just needed a little tighter fit.

As he looked at the box, Tim wondered who came up with the name. He thought the marketing department might want to go back to the drawing board on that one. They probably should remove the word 'Mini,' and while they were at it 'XS' probably wasn't helping them fly off the shelves either. He thought a name like Stealth Extra Super Ultra Snug Fit might improve sales.

With his condoms in sight, Tim used his peripheral vision to check the aisle. When he found he was alone, he snatched the box off the shelf, buried them in his basket and slipped away.

Luckily, the store had one of those self-service checkouts, a key part of Tim's plan. If he were buying Magnums or Durex XLs, he would take them right up to the cashier, but he was cursed with this physical prize and forced to buy his brand in shame.

As Tim struggled with the touch screen at the self-service check out, he noticed an attractive cashier gazing his way. She was obviously bored behind the customer service counter and looking for something, anything, to do. Tim was pleading for the register to just work and for the girl to just not notice him, but it wouldn't and she did. The touch screen refused to respond and he quickly looked around for a register manned by a 'safe' cashier where he could take his sensitive purchase. Tim's ideal cashier would be a seventy year-old man with such bad cataracts that actually seeing what he was scanning would be near impossible.

"Is that register acting up again?" the cashier called to him, smiling.

Tim looked up a little flustered, praying that the comment was not directed toward him. When he located the source, he mumbled an obscenity, grit his teeth and gave her half a smile. "I think I almost have it."

"I can take you right here," the girl said.

Tim went back to pushing the touch screen, but it remained unresponsive. He looked up to the girl again and she was giving him a *what the hell are you waiting for* look. He quickly looked around at his other options, which were semi-full checkout lines manned by hot, but grumpy looking young women and easily made his choice. He picked up the basket containing the condom box and approached the customer service counter. Everything felt like it was in slow motion as he made his way to this smiling cashier. What the hell was she smiling at, he thought? She couldn't be actually enjoying this job. Maybe she saw his attempted purchase and was looking forward to sharing this story with her coworkers.

She was pretty enough, not drop dead you-can-never-touch-me gorgeous, but certainly pretty in a kind of sweet way. As soon as he reached the counter, Tim stole a quick glance at her lower half and noticed that her body was a little curvier than he generally liked. He placed his basket down and began pulling the items out and placing them in front of her. Her nametag read "Emily." Emily picked up the shaving cream and scanned it, then looked at him as if she all of a sudden recognized him and said, "You kind of look familiar." She paused, then added, "Wait... haven't I seen you at MacGrubey's Pub?"

Tim pulled the remaining items out of the basket and arranged them in such a way that the condom box was hidden from her view. "Uh, yeah, I go there."

One of Emily's coworkers, a woman in her mid-forties, stepped behind the counter and began collecting items to restock. The woman smiled at Tim and he acknowledged her with a nervous nod.

"I knew I recognized you," Emily said as she continued scanning and bagging the items. When she picked up the condoms, she studied the box and her face lit up. "Oh, these are adorable!"

That's not exactly how you want your condoms to be described and this caused Tim to cringe and look around even more nervously. To make matters worse, she didn't stop there: "I've heard of the Magnums, but I didn't know they made these."

He rolled his eyes, sighed, then shot back at her, "Well, they do."

The other woman behind the counter looked over and caught a glimpse of the condoms. She returned to her duties as Emily scanned the box, bagged it, then continued scanning the other items.

"So, *big* weekend planned?" she said with a naughty grin.

He paused and gave her a tired look. "Okay, I'm just trying to get to my girlfriend's place and surprise her. Could you just..." He bit his lip in order to cut himself off from uttering a profanity.

Emily either did not recognize that she was starting to annoy him or chose to ignore it as she joked, "If it's going to be your first time with her, believe me she'll be surprised."

The coworker laughed out loud. Tim glared at Emily. "The surprise is dinner. I'm making dinner, not the..." As he noticed the other woman behind the counter still grinning his way, he looked right at her and said, "Okay Mrs. Jeremy. I'm sure your husband is..." Tim stopped himself again from saying something completely inappropriate.

The women both gave him a quizzical look and he felt the need to clarify. "Ron Jeremy, that famous old super-hung porn star!" The women continued to look at him like they had no idea what he was talking about so Tim shook his head, exhaled deeply and gave them a defeated look.

Emily lost the confused stare and shifted gears back to small talk. "Yeah, I think our society is too focused on size. Don't you?" She widened her eyes and waited for a reply as Tim stared at her, impatiently holding his wallet open. She frowned slightly, then looked at the screen and said, "That's 39.98."

Tim didn't change his expression as he handed over the cash. She returned the change and said quietly, "Look, I was just kidding around. Your secret's safe with me." Then she smiled and handed him the bag. Tim looked at her, gave her a sarcastic nod, then walked away.

Emily glanced back to her co-worker with an unsure look. "You think he got that I was flirting?"

Tim was already out the door.

three - Did she say ten year-old boy or was it eight?

As Tim drove toward Jill's place, he asked himself, *Was she flirting with me?* He didn't bother to answer and quickly got sidetracked trying to picture the perky Emily naked. At first he tried to picture her breasts. He noted they weren't all that big, but he didn't like big ones anyway. And he really didn't like ones with disproportionately giant oversized nipples, where the nipple looked like it was trying to take over the whole breast. He thought there should really be a proper breast to nipple ratio, around ninety to no less than eighty percent breast. When you started heading into fifty-fifty territory, look out because it was not a pretty sight.

He glanced over to the lobsters sitting on the passenger seat and they were barely moving in their plastic container. He felt them glaring at him as if somehow they knew they were sacrificing their lives so he could get a longer than normal blowjob and they weren't happy about it at all. Eating lobster seemed to make Jill extra horny. He didn't know if it was the taste or the texture of it that got her going, but he would get hard just watching the way she ate it. She didn't use a fork, she would eat it with her hands and dip chunks of the succulent white meat in butter and slowly bring them to her mouth. She wouldn't bite it, but would somehow gently let the pieces melt on her warm tongue. The way she did it was truly erotic and he would sometimes get so caught up in watching her eat, that he would forget all about eating his own meal. Once he fed her a piece by hand and she started sucking his fingers into her mouth, causing him to nearly blow his load right at the table. He never tried that again for fear of spoiling a good night of sex.

An average blowjob from Jill would last maybe five minutes, but after the lobster, she would go down on him for at least twenty. The lobster-induced blowjob was the premium Jillian Taylor oral sex act. It wasn't one of those regular crappy ones where she would look Tim in the eye every thirty seconds or so with that, *can I stop now and move onto something less involved* expression. It was a blowjob of unmatched, unbridled enthusiasm. He wasn't sure why this crustacean got her so worked up, but he wasn't complaining and he was looking forward to a long night in bed.

As Tim parked near Jill's apartment, he thought about women and their breast sizes and whether they struggled with the same issues as men did about what was in their pants. He was sure that some did, but that was a whole different story entirely. Women have a few options when it comes to breast size, with some of those options being clearly better than others. If a woman really wanted to find out what it was like to have larger ones, she could simply gain a lot of weight. At least some or maybe even lots of the weight would make it to her breasts. But if you're a guy, gaining a bunch of weight actually makes your penis smaller by increasing the fat pad around it so that it is literally swallowed away.

A woman also has the luxury of getting pregnant in order to enhance her figure, at least temporarily, while a guy certainly doesn't have this option. And then there's surgery, a viable option, although shoving a flimsy bag of potentially hazardous chemicals into your body and sewing them up seems a little dangerous, but not completely out of the question. A guy's surgical option is limited to cutting the damn thing off and then reattaching it farther out on his body for some gain in length, and then injecting it with fat for increased girth. These radical treatments can leave you with a flimsy, mushy mess.

A guy would really have to be desperate to opt for surgery, and Tim wasn't anywhere near that desperate. After all, even with his less than spectacular endowment, he'd been able to deliver orgasms to both his previous girlfriend and Jill on a semi-regular basis; although, it wasn't without a nearly backbreaking and literally all-hands-on-deck effort. He used his tool along with his mouth, both hands and maybe even an occasional foot simultaneously in order to stimulate each and every one of the required female zones in a desperate attempt to pull off what often seemed like the impossible. This often left him with the realization that the female body was like a living breathing Rubik Cube.

Sex for him had become an exhausting full team effort and he was sure that if he packed more size, the rest of the team could take a night off once in a while and let super-cock complete the assignment commando style.

Tim used his key to enter Jill's place and he dropped the grocery bags off on the kitchen counter. He heard the shower running and hoped he could catch a glimpse of his sopping wet girlfriend. He hurried into her bedroom then peeked into the bathroom and caught her just as she was washing her beautiful ass. She had a tiny ass. Tim preferred a girl with not so wide and curvy hips. He felt if that area was small, it stood to reason that something else she had down there also would be small and given his own physical status, everything might fit together a little better.

Jill could not see him as he stood in the doorway admiring her, and he fantasized that he was in there with her. He considered stripping down and popping into the shower to help her wash, but then remembered the time he had gotten himself in trouble by doing just that. Jill hated being surprised and hated even more when the shower door was opened and cold air blasted against her body. She also liked the water temperature boiling lava hot and he could not stand it, especially on his sensitive areas. She was pretty high maintenance and he didn't want to chance ruining their night. So he decided to quietly return to the kitchen, but when he turned, something caught his eye on the night table and he walked over to investigate.

He discovered an incredibly large dildo that was bright pink and realistic looking. The monster must have been over a foot long, at least seven inches around and it sported a huge head. He picked it up, studied it in awe and was shocked to find he could not wrap his hand around it. It was unnaturally thick and he was sure he had not seen it around before. He would have remembered this one since it was breathtakingly large. He wondered if guys really could be this size and for a brief moment he wondered why it was sitting out, but then the shower cut off and he quickly placed it back on the night table and snuck out of the room.

In the kitchen, Tim heard Jill drying her hair as the large pot of water was heating on the stove. While he waited, he watched the two lobsters moving on the counter. He imagined that they were leering at him, as if they were actually mad at him. All he could do was smile and say, "Sorry guys. Lobster makes her horny." Not surprisingly, that was no comfort to them.

As Tim pulled a beer out of the refrigerator he heard the hair dryer turn off and seconds later he heard Jill's cell phone ringing in the bedroom.

She answered it briskly. "Where have you been? Never mind, I don't have much time. He'll be here soon. You've got to help me." She switched her phone to speaker mode and said a little louder, "What do I do?"

Tim took a pull of his beer and could hear the voice of Jill's friend Lisa replying, "Just tell him what you told me - that you can't see him anymore because he has the penis of an eight year-old boy."

When Tim heard this, he began to choke on his beer and brought a hand to his mouth so he didn't spray it all over the kitchen. Once he swallowed, he rushed over to the bedroom door to be in better listening position and he heard Lisa giggling over the speakerphone. "I never said that," Jill snapped.

Lisa said, "What about the time he shaved it completely just like those porn star guys do?"

As Tim closed his eyes, mortified, Jill said, "Okay, that was really creepy. But the point is, I said ten year-old boy."

This correction was no comfort to Tim.

"Maybe you should get rid of that giant vibrator," Lisa said.

"I'll never give up The Emperor."

"You're addicted to it and I doubt that any guy, especially a slightly below average one, could compete with it."

The girls shared a laugh as Tim slumped against the wall, un-amused. Then he heard Jill's footsteps and he rushed off to the living room and collapsed into the sofa as Jill said, "But, it's not just the sex, I want to get married at some point and..."

Jill walked out of the bedroom wearing only a bra and panties. They were nothing special, simple white cotton, but she still looked great. She switched her phone out of speaker mode and put it to her ear. She didn't notice Tim on the sofa as she walked past him and into the kitchen. Tim looked pissed off as she came into view, but then melted at the sight of her gorgeous ass. He even tilted his head to follow her around the corner, but as she disappeared into the kitchen he shook off the smile and his sour look returned.

Jill continued, "I don't want husky, prematurely balding, under-endowed and under-motivated kids. He's set to move in here in a few days. I just can't... I feel horrible, but I can't do it." Tim waited for her to notice the lobsters, and then sure enough she came dashing into the living room. Her mouth dropped at the sight of Tim on her sofa and she whispered into the phone, "I have to call you back."

Tim glared at her then stood and rushed right past her to the kitchen. He grabbed a lobster in each hand and headed to the front door without saying a word. Jill followed him and pleaded, "I... Can we talk about this?"

He stood facing the door and looking down at the lobsters. "Will you get the door?"

Jill walked over, placed a hand on his shoulder and he shrugged her off. She paused looking at him for a brief moment, then she sighed, opened the door and watched as Tim walked out.

four - Lauren and the Doctrine of Promissory Estoppel

Jill was the fourth girl that Tim had sex with during the eight years since he lost his virginity. And one of his only real relationships. Tim's other girlfriend was Lauren, and Tim had fallen for her the instant that he saw her. They met in college, in English class, and felt an instant attraction to one another. Lauren was tall, with short hair, a tight body and a great little ass. She was Tim's type. On their second date they went out to eat and then she came back to his dorm room. Tim gave her a quick tour and then they sat next to each other on the bed with nothing to say. He was terrified. She was almost certainly waiting for him to make a move and after a full minute of silence, she said she had better go.

Tim had missed a lot of opportunities with women, and this was dangerously close to being another one. Basically, Tim was a moron when it came to picking up signals and actually making a move. He enjoyed beating himself up over all of his failures with women and he would play them over and over in his mind just for the fun and torture of it all.

He wasn't sure what came over him, but something did and he leaned in and kissed her. He wasn't a very good kisser, but no one had told him so yet. Lauren didn't kiss him for very long, only thirty seconds or so. Maybe it was because of his lacking skill, but Tim liked to believe that it was because she was so attracted to him that she had to have him right then.

Lauren slipped off the bed and looked into his eyes as she unbuttoned his pants. She pulled them down along with his underwear and his slightly smaller than average penis was more than ready. She didn't seem to mind his size and devoured him with her mouth. This was his first ever blowjob and it was mind-blowingly amazing. And boy was she was enthusiastic. As he looked down at her head bobbing up and down on him, Tim could not believe his luck. Nor could he fathom the incredible feeling of just sitting back and watching while being taken care of like that by a gorgeous girl. He found it to be a truly life changing experience.

She performed what could only be described as award-wining oral sex on him for a long time and he considered returning the favor, but from his non-existent experience in that area, he decided against it. When she stopped pleasing him, she began removing her clothes. Halfway through, Tim decided to help. Then he removed the rest of his clothes and she lay down on the bed. He got up and walked over to his dresser where he kept his condom stash but she called him back, telling him he didn't need it. This would be two firsts for him: a blowjob and sex without a condom. Getting an STD never crossed his mind. He wasn't sure if that was because eighty-seven percent of his blood supply was currently confined to his first-time orally pleased penis, or if it was that she smelled so good and looked so incredible naked. However, pregnancy did occur to him, albeit briefly. But he didn't bother asking if she was on the pill, if she practiced some sort of rhythm method, or if she wanted to have his baby. None of that mattered to him at that point.

He sprang back to bed, climbed on her, slipped it in and when he did, he could not believe the sensation. The feeling was unlike anything he had ever experienced. Tim felt like had just entered the tightest, most perfect pussy on the planet.

That night, they had sex at least four times: on the bed, on the beanbag chair, on the floor when they fell off the beanbag, and then back on the bed. They did it in so many different positions that for a guy who, up until then had only experienced relatively bad missionary position sex in a cramped car, it was incredible.

She was definitely more experienced than he was and on their next date Lauren tried to teach Tim how to perform oral sex on her. He tried hard to please her, but he was always in the wrong place, or using too much or too little pressure. He improved his technique a little during the few more dates they had and later, with other girls, he was convinced that he was finally good at it and that he owed it all to Lauren's teachings.

Tim was immature and needy and Lauren had already been dating someone else when they met, so after a few weeks she grew a little tired of him and decided she did not want to see him anymore. Mostly it was a civil breakup and he somehow convinced her to go out with him one last time. He also managed to get her to agree that this one last date would include sex; not just any sex, it would include amazing 'break-up' sex.

So on this last date they went to dinner, but Lauren had decided at some point beforehand that the sex was probably a bad idea. When she told him, Tim took it well, but he decided to try to change her mind. He was taking a Business Law class that semester where they had recently learned about the Doctrine of Promissory Estoppel. The

Doctrine had to do with oral contracts and how if one party promises something to another party and then changes their mind, if the other party would be harmed in some way by the withdrawal of this promise then the promising party would be in violation of the doctrine and in effect be responsible for any damages that said party would incur because of the broken promise. (Or something like that...)

He may not have had all the details of the doctrine straight, but he did receive an 'A' in the class and it could be argued that a promise of sorts had been made. He wasn't sure she bought the argument, but she found him charming enough during his enthusiastically funny discussion of it all that she re-agreed to the sex.

They returned to his room where Tim hoped to perform so expertly that Lauren would desperately want to continue to see him, but the pressure was too much for him and just moments after she went down on him he lost control and it was over. He then struggled to get hard again and could barely get it halfway there, so he attempted to please her with his newfound oral skills. His performance was less than stellar and when she tapped him out mid-lick, it felt like he was being pulled from the ninth inning of game seven in the World Series. He pretended he didn't feel the first tap and returned back to work on her, but when she tapped him again, it was really over and she got dressed and went home.

Looking back he thought maybe he should have ended it with dinner. Had he agreed that she was right, that the sex was probably a bad idea, he would have had the upper hand. He was charming at the restaurant and he could have left her wanting more. She probably would have come back to him on her own, but after that last experience in the bedroom, there was no chance. And after a couple remaining awkward weeks in class together the semester ended and he never saw her again.

five - You call yourself a penis

As Tim drove home, lobsters at his side, he was surprisingly calm. That is, until he drove past the horse that must have been the inspiration for, or at least related to the horse who was the inspiration for, the phrase "hung like a horse." It was standing just behind a fence that separated the farm from the road. This horse was so huge that at first glance, Tim thought the giant thing might actually be a colt standing under the horse. But no, it was one hundred percent all him. Standing next to super horse-cock horse were two mares that were giving the lucky horse the fuck-me eyes. Tim was not aware that horses could flirt like that, but evidently they could.

Tim rolled his eyes then looked once more and when that horse made eye contact with him, he had the feeling it was mocking him. Somehow the horse knew Tim had just been sent packing because of his little issue, while this horse was about to enjoy the first ever equine threesome.

Tim played back Jill's phone conversation in his head and thought she didn't know at all what she was talking about. He, in fact, was bigger now then he had been at the age of ten; he was sure about that. But maybe she was talking about a normal ten year-old boy. Well in that case, maybe... Oh fuck it, he shook off that line of thinking and tried to focus on Jill's flaws. She didn't have many, at least physically, but he was sure he spotted a hint of a patch of cellulite forming on her ass as she walked past him to the kitchen. At least he would keep telling himself that and with that thought, as shaky grounded as it was, he smiled for the first time all day.

Tim drank himself to sleep that night watching TV in bed as the lobsters swam in a small cooler next to him. After he showered the next morning, Tim examined his thinning hair in the bathroom mirror with a frown. He picked up a pill bottle of ProHairCal, which he had purchased two months before and been taking religiously ever since, and studied the label for a moment.

He mumbled something about the money back guarantee and then tossed the bottle into a drawer and called it worthless crap. Tim dropped his towel and looked himself over in the mirror. He grabbed a handful of belly fat and shook his head in disgust. He wondered how, after just a few years, he could have let himself get so out of shape. He had gained fifteen pounds and most of it seemed to be isolated right in his stomach.

He tried to pull his stomach in, stood tall with his shoulders back and it made him look only marginally better. He smiled thinking that maybe he could get back in shape; that it wouldn't be too hard. And then the smile faded when he looked down and saw it. He bent over a little to get a closer look and it appeared especially small, as if that were even possible. He looked up to the mirror to get another angle on it, the angle that a girl would get when she first caught sight of it and he just scowled as he stared right at the thin, short, tiny, disgrace to all penises everywhere. He looked back down at it, grabbed it with two fingers and turned the head of it up as if it could actually look at him and he said, "And you... You call yourself a penis."

Later, Tim worked out. Well, he considered it a workout, but almost anyone else on the planet would not. He wore only gym shorts and sat on the sofa connected to the AutoXerSizer. The AutoXerSizer is a device that claims to build muscle through electric pulses, and Tim connected himself up to it a few times a week since he was too lazy to actually do real, heart-pumping exercises. It was a simple looking device with only a single knob with settings from zero through ten. Pads ran from the device to Tim's chest, biceps, stomach and thighs. The device hummed gently as Tim turned the dial up to five and sat back comfortably watching television.

During these less than grueling routines, he would enjoy a beer, but at least it was a light beer. He would also consume his cocktail of supplements during these sessions, and he proceeded to swallow a HydroDragenX pill, designed to burn fat, and the hair pill, which he was convinced did not work, but was taking anyway, with a swig of beer.

As Tim was enjoying the gentle pulses from the AutoXerSizer, his cell phone rang. He didn't bother to check the display. Instead, he took another sip of beer and then something caught his eye on television.

The spot started with Bill, an unconscious man being rushed into a hospital on a gurney by two female paramedics. Bill was wearing only a towel. The voiceover for the commercial announced, "Bill's not having a good day."

A female doctor and nurse began to work on Bill while the paramedics looked on with concern and the first paramedic said, "He was found unresponsive at the gym on the floor of the sauna. Possible heart attack, pulse 140, BP 50 over 30."

The medical professionals lifted Bill from the gurney to the table and in the process Bill's towel fell open. The doctor attached monitors to Bill's chest and began to examine him. A heart monitor started to beat slowly. A nurse prepared to insert an IV into Bill's hand, but after she glanced at his groin, she got instantly sidetracked and began to laugh as she stared at Bill's crotch.

The other three women quickly focused on what the nurse found so amusing and began to smile. Then they looked to one another and giggled. The heart monitor flat lined as the women laughed uncontrollably.

The commercial voiceover began, "Bill's mother always told him to wear clean underwear just in case he ever got into an accident. We believe it's more important to take MaxiManhood... just in case."

Then the scene rewound to the nurse preparing to insert the IV and getting sidetracked, but this time she stared at Bill's groin open-mouthed. One by one the other three women followed the preoccupied nurse's gaze. The room was now silent with all four women focused on Bill's groin. The women stared with their eyes widening. One even slowly and seductively licked her lips. The heart monitor flat lined and alarms went off in the room, snapping the women to attention.

The nurse jumped on the man's lap and began chest compressions. The doctor grabbed a hand-held resuscitator, looked at Bill then tossed it behind her and put her lips to his to perform mouth-to-mouth.

The scene now cut to a conscious Bill sitting up in bed glowing as the four women happily fawned over him with the voiceover, "Try MaxiManhood risk free. Guaranteed to make you at least 30% larger and it could just save your life. Try MaxiManhood and be all you were meant to be."

Tim watched the commercial, mesmerized, and when it was over he reached for his phone. It might have been that the AutoXerSizer was turned up too high, or maybe it was the beer. It could have been the supplements, or the combination of it all, but whatever it was, Tim was excited to place his order; so much so that he upgraded to expedited shipping.

six - Brandi Nicole's Double Adventure

Tim tried to sleep, but his mind was racing. He started thinking about the MaxiManhood commercial and then started to have second thoughts about his order. He considered calling and trying to cancel it, but that would be infinitely more embarrassing than when he placed it in the first place. He shook off that thought and started wondering if there was a chance that the pill actually worked. He could be like those guys in porn who were huge - the kind of guys women drooled over. He started playing back in his head some of his favorite porn movie scenes. He flashed back to the old days, like ten years ago when you had to actually load up a DVD to watch one. What a pain that was. And to switch to another movie you needed to unload the one disk and load another and wait to get through all the menu crap. He wondered how he'd survived.

From the moment he discovered online video on demand, in his sophomore year of college, Tim's life changed for the better. He believed that video on demand was by far the greatest gift that the Internet had delivered to mankind. That groundbreaking porn miracle allowed him to skip around and preview vast numbers of films, without committing to watching the entire masterpiece, while he searched for that one special scene that would get him off. Tonight, he focused in on films featuring men with large-sized packages (which weren't difficult to find), in order to prepare himself for the changes that would soon occur below his belt. He wasn't expecting to stumble across the name Brandi Nicole, a name he hadn't thought of in years. It was simply too painful. Although never his girlfriend, hell, Tim had never even met the woman, Brandi Nicole had been Tim's first love.

Brandi was the star of a porn movie he'd discovered during one of his marathon video on demand sessions. Okay, so maybe she wasn't the star, but she was in one of the scenes. A mostly tame scene, for porn anyway, where the girl looked gorgeous and a little shy and had mostly normal super-passionate sex with one guy; it wasn't one of those gangbang scenes or anything like that. For the most part, it was tastefully done and Tim watched open-mouthed as Brandi gracefully performed and he instantly fell for her.

In his mind, Tim imagined that this was Brandi's first and only porn film. He assured himself that she had done only that one scene and then she was out of the business. He imagined that her costar was probably her boyfriend at the time and she did the movie only to earn money for her college tuition. He thought Brandi was the kind of girl you could bring home; just throw some clothes on her and you'd have no trouble introducing her to mom. He watched the scene over and over, never growing tired of it and always 'finishing' right along with her. They were so in sync it was remarkable, if not disturbing. Tim's infatuation with Brandi grew until one lonely night when Tim decided to Google his love and then his world came crashing down. After searching a few other sites, he found out that this was not her one and only film. She had in fact been in a few more films; seventy-seven to be exact. Most of the titles were so vile that he cringed just reading them.

He watched a few seconds of each of her scenes. He would watch until the disgust of witnessing his future wife perform such depraved acts with unattractive, filthy-looking men overtook him and forced him to quickly close the offending window on his computer and move to the next one.

Things went from bad to worse when Tim viewed the crown jewel in Brandi's film career. Tim had never before seen anyone do this, nor did he know it was even remotely possible and he found that witnessing your future wife doing it was actually the very worst possible way to be exposed to the shocking act. The offending film carried a particularly anal-centric title and Brandi was definitely the star. Her big scene involved two hideously unattractive men where she was the recipient of what in the porn business carries the name "double anal." If you are unfamiliar with the term, it kind of means what you think it means. Double as in two and anal as in the place where not even a single one is really supposed to be. Tim watched the scene unfold in horror. It was formally the end of their non-existent relationship.

It was a full week before Tim was able to stomach watching porn on the Internet, and it wasn't until many, many, weeks later that Tim was able to fully enjoy it again.

Whenever Tim thought of Brandi, it reminded him of a joke he'd heard from a comedian hosting the AVN Awards, which is the adult film industries version of the Academy Awards. Except in the AVN awards, they recognize actresses in slightly racier categories, like best blowjob, best girl on girl, and best anal scene. The comedian was addressing a group of porn stars and the joke was about how everyone in the crowd was enjoying double anal while the comedian still struggled just to get single vaginal. Tim also struggled with single vaginal. The joke was a hit with the crowd and was still funny to Tim, but it also gave him a pang. He felt that when the audience laughed, they were laughing at him.

His remembrances of Brandi, painful as they were, still got him worked up. It had been a long time since he had thought about her. And maybe a small part of him still had feelings for her - a really small part. He reached down and felt that he was incredibly hard. Tim got out of bed, went to the bathroom and jerked off, hoping that it would help put him to sleep. As he watched himself in the mirror he hoped that it would be one of the few remaining times he'd have to work with such small equipment.

seven – Don't fuck with me or those rubber bands go right back on

On Monday morning, still feeling the sting of being recently dumped, Tim laid awake in bed with an open cooler nearby, half-filled with water and the lobsters. The alarm rang and he turned it off. He looked over at the dormant lobsters, concerned and said, "Are you still with me? Guys?"

After tapping the cooler and still getting no response, he reached in the water, a lobster snapped its claw at him, and he pulled his hand away quickly and said, "Hey. Don't fuck with me or those rubber bands go right back on."

Tim arrived for work that day a few minutes late, just as he always did. The company was a casual place and his job as a developer in the Information Technology group was not terribly taxing. The most stressful thing he ever dealt with was an occasional late night support call and in return he was afforded some flexibility in his schedule.

As Tim opened the door to the lobby, he looked back to find Kelly approaching along with another woman. Kelly was in her mid-twenties, attractive, super-model tall, and one of the two women at the company that Tim often fantasized about. The women approached slowly as they were engrossed in conversation and oblivious to the fact that Tim was graciously waiting and holding the door.

Kelly said to the woman, "I'm serious. You can't miss the next happy hour. I'm not even kidding."

Tim kept looking up to make eye contact with Kelly, but it never happened, so Tim simply said, "Hey." But there was no response from either of the women as they walked right past him without any acknowledgement of his existence. Tim stood for a second and looked up to the sky, then rushed to catch up with them in the lobby. The women scanned their ID cards, the automatic turnstiles opened, and they walked through as Tim called after them, "Hey, when's the next one?"

Both women looked back at him, bothered, as Tim struggled to scan his ID card. That card never worked correctly for him and he meant to get a new one, but never got around to it. Tim, still barred from reaching them by the turnstiles and with a goofy look on his face added, "See, I'm a recently free man, so..."

The women shared a look as his ID card struggle continued. "That's amazing. I'll let you know," Kelly said as she and the woman disappeared around the corner, giggling.

Just before noon, Tim and Carter headed to their lunchtime basketball game. They played a few times a week. On days they played, they ended up out of the office a little longer than what a traditional lunch hour allowed, but mostly upper management looked the other way, and sometimes even joined in the games. Carter was Tim's age, his coworker and best friend. Carter was not terribly good looking or outgoing, and he didn't do particularly well with women. Somehow none of it bothered him. Carter rarely complained. He was simply comfortable in his own skin; he was the polar opposite of Tim.

Then there was Rick. Rick never missed a basketball game or a chance to screw with Tim. He was a muscular, super obnoxious douche twenty-five year old who made Tim's life hell both on and off the court. Rick was really well endowed and he didn't care who knew about it. Actually, he wanted everyone to know about it. At the age of ten, he was hung like most normal guys were at twenty. His nickname was Rick the Dick, mostly because he was a giant asshole, but also because of his giant, mutant-sized penis. For the most part he treated girls like garbage, but almost all of them came back for more. He's what most guys refer to as a fucking lucky bastard.

As Tim and Carter walked down the hall they approached Rick, who currently had Rachael cornered in the hallway. He was standing a little too close to her, as was evident from that *'get me the hell out of here'* look on her face, which Rick was clearly oblivious to.

Rachael Adams, also twenty-five, was attractive and always upbeat. She was the other girl in the office that Tim longed for.

As Tim and Carter approached Rick and Rachael, Tim whispered, "There she is."

Rick leaned in even closer to Rachael, gave her a skeptical look and said, "What could you possibly be doing?"

"Uh, I'm having lunch tomorrow with..." She paused and then caught site of Tim approaching and backed away from Rick and said, "Tim, there you are." She slipped past Rick, escaped to Tim and touched him on the arm. Tim looked at her hand, blissfully, then into her eyes, open-mouthed and a little pathetic. She said to Tim, "Are we still on for lunch tomorrow?"

Rick eyed them both suspiciously. Tim looked at Rick, then at Rachael as she gave him the play-along eyes. Carter looked at Tim like he was a moron, as Rachael added, "Tomorrow?"

After a beat, the lights finally came on for Tim and he struggled to get out, "Uh. Yeah, sure. The lunch thing."

Rick narrowed his eyes, glared at Rachael and said to the guys, "See you two on the court." Then Rick headed around the corner, took a few steps down the hall and quietly waited, eavesdropping on the three.

Rachael turned to be sure Rick was gone then looked back to Tim. "I can't stand that creep. He has the nerve to ask me to lunch after he dumped this complaining customer on me. I shouldn't have to do his work. I called the customer and followed up with an email. I was just trying to help and I got back this nasty email..." She paused and looked like she might be on the verge of tears then continued, "I don't need to be treated like I'm some kind of moron. I don't need this crap today. I was already having a bad day before this so I just--"

Tim said, "What'd you do?"

"So, I kinda lost it and wrote this awful reply. It made me feel so much better."

Tim said, "Wait, you didn't send it, right?"

Rachael, said, "Oh, no. It's still in my drafts folder. I could never send it, but it felt so good to write. You know?"

Around the corner, Rick had heard everything. He smiled as he slipped away.

Tim gave her a reassuring nod. He'd never seen her anything but happy. She seemed so vulnerable at that moment and he just wanted to wrap his arms around her and tell her it would be okay and then maybe take her to his apartment for a few hours and.... Tim began to daydream as Carter said something comforting to her, which Tim was too wrapped up in his own thoughts to hear.

Carter and Rachael continued their conversation and as she laughed at something Carter had said, Tim interrupted, "So, lunch tomorrow?"

"Oh, you don't have to. Well, unless you really want to," Rachael replied and smiled at him sweetly.

But he was like a deer-in-headlights, frozen. He finally said, "Oh. No, okay so no then."

Carter stared at him, disappointed yet again, as Rachael gave him a strange look. "We'd better get going," Tim mumbled.

Rachael said, "Okay, thanks again. You saved me." She paused for an awkward silent moment and looked at Tim, then turned and disappeared around the corner. Carter elbowed Tim in the side. Tim grimaced then rolled his eyes in the knowledge of what a complete fucking moron he really was.

eight - Don't look at my junk

Tim and Carter stood on opposite sides of Carter's car. Carter just stared at him as Tim attempted to open the locked door. Tim gave him an impatient look and said, "What?"

With a vacant stare and in his best moron voice, Carter said, "Okay, so no lunch then."

Tim returned a look conceding that he was an absolute idiot.

Carter said, "She's hot, clearly digging you and practically begging you to bone her?"

They both climbed in the car. Carter started the engine while still shaking his head in disbelief.

"How do you know she wants to bone me?"

"It's the way she was touching your arm."

"I know. She was," Tim said smiling.

Carter backed out of the parking space. Tim looked at him, dejected and said, "But what if she's like Jill and only wants a guy with a huge dick?"

"You never know. Maybe she likes guys with pathetically small dicks."

Tim gave him a tired look. "Thank you."

As Carter drove, Tim played back in his mind some of his more famous drop-the-ball moments where he let slip away absolutely guaranteed sex. Once a girl slept over his college dorm suite the night before they were to take a trip to the beach together. That night they went to a bar together and then back to his place. The semester had not yet started, and he had a three-bedroom suite all to himself. But instead of setting her up in his bed or at the very least putting her in the lower bunk in his room, where one thing most certainly would have led to another, he set her up in a separate room which resulted in absolutely nothing happening that night.

Here you had a girl who was A-probably drunk, B-agreed to a sleep over at your place, and C-agreed to accompany you the next day on an overnight trip. Now most guys, at this point, would be checking their condom supply and be planning how to make their move, but not Tim; he was inept when it came to this sort of thing. To make matters worse, a few minutes after he put her to bed, she came to his room and woke him up. She stood just inside the door and told him that she was confused by the situation. When Tim didn't respond, she asked him flat out why he had never made a move on her. When he groggily replied, "I'm not sure," she sighed and returned to her room.

The next morning she gave him one last chance as she showered with the door to the bathroom partially open. That was a hint and a half for his ass to join her, but he spent so much time contemplating what exactly the open door meant that by the time he mustered up the balls to go for it, she cut off the water, which sent him running back to his room. So that was not one, but two missed opportunities with the same girl within eight hours. It does a disservice to the word opportunity to even call those completely un-subtle absolutely guaranteed invitations for sex, opportunities. Tim blew it that night, big time.

There were also multiple occurrences of Tim ending up in girl's dorm rooms and simply sitting with them in silence on their beds until the girls finally called it a night and sent him away. No matter how many times Tim vowed to never let those kinds of things happen again, they always did.

As they pulled into the parking lot of the gym, Tim shook off these memories, which he had always been too embarrassed to share with anyone.

Minutes later on the basketball court, Tim and Carter stood together as five guys took warm up shots and Tim said, "I'm going to do it. I'm going to ask her out."

Carter rolled his eyes and he and Tim both watched Rick as he made his entrance onto the court, decked out in overpriced compression wear. When Rick ran past Tim, he said, "Try to give us a game today, biaaaaatch." Rick actually somehow managed to pronounce all the "A's" in the obscure slang form of that word. With the extended pronunciation, it took him about five seconds to get it all out. This was his signature, and he was strangely proud of it, even though it couldn't have been more annoying to the rest of the planet.

During the first game, Rick caught a pass and nailed one from long range and afterward Tim and Carter shared a tired look as Rick shouted, "That's what I'm talkin' 'bout!"

During the second game, Tim had a good position between Rick and the basket. Rick got a pass, backed up, plowed right over Tim, knocked him to the ground and hit the shot. Rick looked down at Tim and said, "Eat-it biaaaaatch." Tim glared back at him as the other guys headed down the court. Rick said, mocking him in a baby voice, "Do you wanna call a foul?"

During the third game, Carter passed the ball to Tim who, with Rick out of position, was wide open for the shot. Tim hesitated, contemplating his next move long enough for Rick to be all over him. He panicked and attempted to pass the ball but Rick tipped it away, knocking it to one of his teammates who passed it back to Rick, breaking for an easy lay up. Tim turned away, dejected.

Carter gave Tim a sarcastic, "Nice."

After the games, Tim and Carter sat on the bench in the locker room as Rick stood nude, unabashedly facing them and uncomfortably close, while the five other sweaty guys got undressed facing their lockers. Tim and Carter struggled to maintain eye contact with Rick as he put everything out for display.

As Rick bragged about his on-court performance, Tim just had to steal a look at Rick's junk and when he did, it pissed him off. He wondered how the fuck an asshole like Rick was blessed with that thing. Life wasn't fair and that thing was freaking scary. Tim sighed, turned away from the monstrosity and started searching through his gym bag. As he searched for absolutely nothing, he became lost in thought. He admitted that he spent a slightly inordinate amount of time comparing himself to other guys; it was bordering on an obsession. Maybe it was silly, he realized that, but he couldn't help himself. He wondered if maybe he'd watched too much porn in his life. No one should really see that many penises, should they? All those close ups of the action kind of get burned in your brain. When you close your eyes, you sometimes see people going at it and you aren't one of them and that can't be good for anybody. And they didn't hire average guys for those films; they use maybe the top four percent of the population. Watching all that professional on-screen humping would make anyone feel inadequate and end up with a false perception of what is normal.

Tim glanced back at Rick just as Rick said, "You guys sucked again today."

"Could you maybe back up a little?" Tim begged.

"What, is this body too tempting for you? Bringing out all those confused feelings."

"Did you ever mature past the age of 13?" Tim said.

"At least my dick did," Rick said, cracking himself up.

When Tim failed to react, Rick continued, "So why the fuck are you hitting on Rachael, when you've got Jill?"

"We broke up."

This brought a smile to Rick's face and Tim glared at him. "What?"

"I'll never understand how you got her in the first place," Rick said, as he looked Tim over from head to toe, briefly stopping at Tim's groin and shaking his head, frowning. "How will she ever find another guy to fill your shoes?" Then he turned and walked off to the showers, laughing as Tim flipped him off.

Carter gave Tim a sympathetic look and said, "The only thing bigger than his dick is his ego."

Tim sighed. "He's such a douche."

A few minutes later as Tim, Carter and another guy showered, Rick grabbed his towel from the hook and began drying himself off. Tim looked down at his own penis and thought about how incredibly small it looked at that moment. He was sure that it had never before looked so thin; it was as if it was trying to disappear right before his eyes. Maybe it was that damn cold water. Super dickhead Rick must have used more than his fair share of hot water, which only made sense since he had way more than his fair share of both penis size and douchebaggy'ness. Tim glanced at Rick and caught him smirking his way and checking him out below the belt. Then Rick wrapped the towel around his neck and just stood there with his package on display as he looked down and admired his own six-pack abs.

Tim and Carter rolled their eyes while they watched as Rick tried unsuccessfully to pinch fat on his stomach. Then Rick gave Tim an arrogant look and said, "No refined sugar since 2002. You should try it."

Tim replied, "Thanks, but I've kinda got, uh, my own regiment going on."

Rick narrowed his eyes, nodded with a grin and turned to go.

nine - Pumping, jelqing, hanging and other penile torture

Back at work, Tim attended a meeting with Bev Lawson, a tough as nails executive in her late fifties who thought she was still super sexy, but if she ever was, it was twenty years and thirty pounds ago. Bev sat agitated, as she did at every meeting, at a table along with Tim's boss George, Tim, and a few others.

Tim continued, "So, I thought that might help. You see we--" and was cut off by Bev, who never tried to hide her disdain for Tim.

"We've been over this time and again," she said. "Look, my people cannot take on any more manual work. Are we clear?"

"No, I think you misunderstand--"

"No, I think I got it," Bev snapped back.

George said, "Hold on a second Bev." George then leaned over and said quietly to Tim, "Go draw it up on the board," as Bev looked on impatiently.

Tim whispered back to George, "No. She'll just--"

With way too much volume, Bev said, "Is there anything else?"

George gave Tim a disappointed look, paused, then said, "No."

After the others had left the room, Tim sat rubbing the bridge of his nose, still dazed from his scolding as George looked on. George said, "Why didn't you draw it out for her?"

"She hates me. She never would've gone for it."

"Yeah, she definitely hates you, but you better win her over. You'll never move up here until you do."

Back at his desk Tim hung up the phone and crossed off an ad in the newspaper apartment listings, just as Carter burst into his office holding a post-it note. Carter closed the door and Tim looked at him, distraught.

Carter said, "Dude, good news and bad news. First, I hate to tell you this, but your girlfriend Rachael was fired... over that email thing, she--"

"No way," Tim burst.

"Yep, about 30 minutes ago."

"And I was all set to ask her out."

Carter gave him a skeptical look.

Tim exhaled deeply, "Shit."

Carter looked at the post-it note then said, "Okay, the good news. I think I have a solution to your little problem, or at least a couple of things you could try."

Tim gave Carter a confused look, as he was still a little preoccupied thinking about Rachael.

Carter noticed Tim's look and said, "You know, your problem..."

"Oh yeah."

Carter added, "Did you know there was so much information about penis enlargement on the Internet?"

"Well, duh."

"When you Google penis enlargement, you get like 8 million hits," Carter said wide-eyed.

"I know. I know," Tim said, giving him a look that

said get to it already.

"Anyway, I found a couple things," Carter said.

"Really what?"

"Have you heard of jelqing?"

"Tried it."

"A penis pump?"

"Have one."

"Pills?"

"Tried a few. They do nothing."

Carter looked at him, a little disappointed, then he glanced back down to the post-it note, scowled and said hesitantly, "Uh, something called hanging?"

"Saw it online, never tried it. It looks really painful," Tim said, feeling like a penile enlargement expert and proud of it.

Carter narrowed his eyes as if he were amazed that Tim was already aware of or had personal experience with all these methods.

Tim shook his head at Carter and said, "This can't be the first time you've heard of all of this stuff?"

"It is. Why would I know any of this?"

"I don't know. You're a guy aren't you? Are you huge or something?"

"I'm not sure."

Tim gave him a confused look. "I mean, in comparison to porn guys are you?"

"I don't watch porn."

"Never?" Tim asked.

"Maybe once in high school. It did nothing for me."

"So what are your numbers?"

"What... what numbers?"

"Length and girth. What are they?" Tim demanded curtly.

"Of my dick?" Carter choked.

"No, your biceps." Tim rolled his eyes. "Yes of your dick. Maybe you don't know the girth, that's understandable, but you have to--"

"The girth? As in how big around it is?"

"Yes, exactly. How thick it is," Tim repeated, with a smile on his face meant to imply that he knew Carter was screwing around with him.

Carter looked around and dropped his voice. "How the heck do you measure the girth?"

"With one of those seamstress tape measures," Tim replied, as if it were obvious.

"Why do you have one of those?" Carter asked.

"I just do, alright?"

"Well I don't *have* a seamstress tape measure, so the answer is no. I've never measured the girth."

"Okay, so the length, you have to know the length. Come on. There are like, two guys on the planet that haven't measured their dicks. Like maybe the Pope and the Dalai Lama. Okay make that one guy. You never know with the priests, some really like to party," Tim said.

Carter shook his head. "I can't believe we're even talking about this. It's a little gay."

"You brought it up. This is what guys do," Tim retorted, trying to sound casual.

"Yeah, maybe in prison."

"I'm not asking to jerk you off or anything. It's not gay. So, you must know the length?"

"No, I don't."

"You're serious?"

"Yes. I. Have. Never. Measured. It. Okay?" Carter mouthed the words slowly while performing made up hand signing.

Tim shook his head in disbelief, opened his mouth to say something, but had nothing.

Carter looked at him, perplexed. "Why would anyone measure it?"

"Why wouldn't anyone?" Tim asked, and when he realized Carter was not going to answer, he continued his interrogation. "Okay, so what kind of condoms do you buy?"

"What's that got to do with anything?" Carter was losing patience.

"I mean, what size - the Magnums or the regular-sized ones?"

"The regular ones," Carter replied.

"Uh huh. And you've never even thought about what it would be like to be bigger?"

"Why would I? I'm secure. I'm satisfied. And any woman who is into me for worthwhile reasons is satisfied." Carter looked at Tim like he was missing the obvious. "Don't you get it? Size doesn't matter."

Tim just stared at him. "Who are you, Oprah? Most guys are obsessed with the size of their dicks. Even if it's like ten inches long, you still want it to be a foot."

Carter shrugged.

"It never crossed your mind?" Tim asked, but didn't wait for a reply. "You're not normal!"

"Why? Because I'm not upset that I'm not wearing mutant-sized condoms? Because I'm not pining away searching for some miracle dick enlargement solution? If I was, that would make me a normal guy?"

"Yes." Tim paused for a moment, looked away, then back to Carter. "No, I mean..."

"Maybe it's you who isn't normal," Carter said confidently.

"Okay, so maybe I have a slight problem. But somewhere between where I am and where you are is a normal guy."

"All right, I'll give you that," Carter said, then he lowered his voice. "You really know your numbers?"

"I do."

Carter shook his head in disbelief, but let it go, then glanced back to his post-it note and asked, "So what's this jelqing thing?"

Tim answered matter-of-factly, "Jelqing is the art of absolutely beating the shit out of your penis by pulling on it, stretching it, and bending it while in various states of erection. It really fucking hurts and you can damage it permanently. There are these lists of exercises. One is where you pull it out from your body while you're completely soft, as far as it will go, and hold it that way for like thirty seconds. I tried the routines only a few times. I think the goal is to gain like, a quarter inch of scar tissue. But you can really screw it up and it will just stop working. So I would say don't do it."

"And the penis pump?" Carter asked.

"It's a tube that you stick your dick in and then a vacuum seal is created and you squeeze the trigger to suck the air out of the tube and pull more blood into your dick to pump it up..." Tim narrowed his eyes and continued, "You ever get one of those blow jobs from a girl and it seemed pretty good at the time, but felt a little different, like she was... doing something wrong? But it felt pretty good, so you let her do her thing and then the next day your dick really hurt and was like red in a few spots?"

Carter nodded as if he had been there at least once before.

Tim continued, "All right, well, that girl didn't know what the hell she was doing and she was actually sucking. I know they call it sucking cock, but you're not supposed to actually suck it too much. What happened was that chick burst some blood vessels in your dick."

"You should change careers, go into urology," Carter joked.

"Well, pumping... it is like that, except it hurts all over and instead of hurting for a couple of days, the pain lasts for like two weeks. Oh, and if you pump it up too much, you can end up with a freakish donut ring around your dick, like a tire tube."

Carter appeared overwhelmed from all Tim's complex explanations.

Tim smiled and said, "It looks really cool and big while in the tube, but once you pull it out it shrinks back down to normal. Not to mention you could really mess up your shit. You could break something in there and never be able to get a boner again."

Carter said, "Then why do guys do all this shit?"

Tim paused, exhaled deeply then said, "Do we really have to go through this again?"

"No, please don't." Carter looked sickened by the penis conversation. He crumpled up the post-it and tossed it into the trash. He grabbed the newspaper from Tim's desk and asked, "Find anything?"

"No and they already rented my place. I've got to be out Thursday." Tim stared down at his desk.

"My couch is still available."

"Thanks, but I'm not sleeping on your cat's litter box."

"She only pissed there twice. I turned over the cushion and the smell is almost completely gone."

Tim rolled his eyes and the two shared a laugh. Then Tim said, "I've got too much stuff, anyway. I never thought I'd do it, but I'll just have to move back home for a while."

ten - What the hell is a Feng Shui retreat?

Ted and Connie Garrett were Tim's semi-loving parents. They maintained the five-bedroom family home that they had purchased when Tim and his older sister were in elementary school. Ted had put in a pool for the family about ten years ago and the couple still enjoyed it. Although the empty nesters didn't need all the space, they decided to keep the house anyway. This was especially surprising since once the kids moved out, the couple removed pretty much any evidence that they actually had kids. Other than a few well-hidden pictures, you wouldn't have known this middle-aged couple had ever procreated.

But it wasn't until they became grandparents that they truly snapped. Their daughter had given birth to a beautiful baby girl more than two years ago, and the pair had developed inventive ways to avoid babysitting. They had even missed some of the child's major life events, like a birthday and a Baptism, without any valid excuse other than needing to catch an episode of *The Amazing Race*.

Soon after they became the dreaded 'G' word, they quickly transformed the house into one of the most non-child proof residences on the planet. A house that no parent in their right mind would ever leave their young. Glass tables and breakable knick-knacks were everywhere, along with a number of super fragile, incredibly expensive large grandfather clocks that emitted nap-killing chimes every hour on the hour. Bowls of tiny decorative infant choking rocks seemed to be in every room. Tim was sure that if you searched hard enough you might just find a fork lying next to an unprotected electrical outlet, which might also be next to a plastic bag labeled, 'keep away from children.' These two had done their time. They had raised their kids and had absolutely no interest in being grandparents, and they made no effort to hide it.

After work Tim sat with his parents, both dressed a little too young for their age, at a table on the patio near the in-ground pool. They were enjoying a cocktail while Tim pleaded his case and asked to move back in, at least temporarily. Actually he really didn't ask, it was more like he assumed he could move right back in with them. What child would ever think he was not welcomed back at the family home? But Tim wasn't welcome, and it was clearly written on their faces. After he announced his intentions, Ted and Connie looked at each other with concern, then paused and slowly shifted their gaze to Tim.

"You can't move back in," Ted said.

"What? Why?" Tim said, shocked.

Connie said with an unashamed, confident nod, "We need our privacy," and Ted nodded along in complete agreement.

"But, Becky was here till she was like, 25, and I left when I started college."

Ted said, "I know. And we're finally free."

Tim looked at his father, then his mother, then back and forth between each of them with a slight grin, as he thought he was being played. But when their expressions didn't change, he exhaled deeply and slumped back in his chair.

Ted held firm and added, "Look, you can stay, but just until we get back from the cruise."

Connie said, "Sleep on the pull out."

"What about my room?"

His parents looked at each other, scrambling for the words. Ted paused and said, "We, uh, turned that it into a relaxation slash massage--"

"A what?" Tim interrupted.

"It's more of a Feng Shui retreat. They're really popular now. But, don't go in there. It's really a mess. It's still a work in progress," Connie said as Tim eyed them both suspiciously.

"But what about the guest room?" Tim whined.

"That's for your mother's scrap booking, and your sister's room is now my office. We put all the beds in storage," Ted said.

"I'll just set up my bed in the--"

Connie lifted her hand up as if she'd had enough conversation on the subject, "You shouldn't go to all that trouble when you'll just be moving out."

Tim looked stricken and a little dizzy from the ping-pong rapid-fire parental tag team, but it wasn't over.

"We were just crazy about Jill," Ted added switching gears with a cheery look on his face.

"She was such a fabulous girl," Connie said.

"How the hell did you screw that up?"

"She was so good for you, Tim. You were a complete mess before you met her." Connie shook her head slowly in disappointment.

Tim opened his mouth to speak, nothing came out. His parents almost seemed happy that he had screwed it up. He eyed them strangely then sighed deeply and said, "I just wasn't... She was looking for something that I just couldn't give her."

Tim swore he saw his parents quickly grin at each other, as if they shared some kind of inside joke on the subject. Then they looked back to Tim, who narrowed his eyes at them, a little creeped out by the exchange.

Connie said, "Now if she thinks you need to change, then she's probably right."

"I'm working on it," Tim said and he let his forehead fall on the table, completely defeated.

As the elder Garrett was walking Tim back to his car, they stopped in front of the open garage. Inside were an SUV and a sporty little BMW Z4 Roadster. Ted stood and admired his sports car as Tim looked out over the front yard of the house he grew up in and spotted the large tree he once attempted to climb and promptly fell out of. The neighborhood was going through some changes now. Like the Garretts, many of the families' kids were now gone, but unlike the Garretts, most of those parents had decided to sell. Some of the houses had sold and younger couples had moved in, but several houses were still for sale; some had been on the market for more than a year.

Tim looked around at the four houses that were visible from the lawn and noticed that two had for-sale signs. "What's with everybody selling?"

"This real estate meltdown. It's destroying the neighborhood," Ted said.

Tim looked suspiciously at the white house across the street which had a no-trespassing sign in a first floor window and a garden hose coming out of a second floor window. The hose ran from the window into the woods next to the house. Despite Ted and Connie's repeated wishes, this house was not one of the properties currently available for sale in the neighborhood.

Tim said, "Did you call the police again about that house?"

"Yeah and they haven't done a thing. Cars come and go at odd hours. No one over there works. Something's definitely going on."

Ted returned to eyeing his prized BMW and squinted when he thought he spotted an imperfection. He moved closer. "Ah, thank God. It was only a shadow."

Tim thought if he drove a car like that, he might be able to get away with being even less endowed than he already was and still manage to get laid. Tim walked over to the car and looked at it mesmerized. "I could drive her while you're gone. I read you should drive a car at least once a week or--"

"No, don't. It'll be fine," Ted shot back.

Tim opened the door, climbed in, sat in the driver's seat and gazed at the dash as his father looked on with growing concern.

Ted said, "I know the mileage."

As Tim drove away, he thought about what an ass his father was. Ted had never let him drive his precious sports cars. Every couple of years Ted would replace his current hot car with a newer and more expensive one. Back in the late 80s there was a 380ZX, and there must have been five or six cars since then. Now it was this little BMW convertible. Never once did Ted hand down or offer to sell his son his old model, at a good family discounted price of course. Instead, he traded them in secretly and would just reappear, out of the blue, with a shiny and more expensive new one. He wondered if Ted had always driven those types of cars to compensate for some little personal flaw; a personal flaw that he had, in fact, passed down to his only son.

Tim wondered if you inherit that from your father's side, or if it's from the men on your mother's side? Or is that baldness, or does that skip a generation, or... Screw it. Ted was probably sporting a tiny one and that was why he drove what he drove. He was over-compensating for something, and Tim thought he knew exactly what it was. He wondered why he was even thinking about this. What if he somehow found out that he actually did inherit his father's pathetic penis? The idea made him nauseous. He tried to erase these wild thoughts from his mind, but it was too late. They would stick with him for quite a while.

eleven - It seemed like a good idea at the time

Tim returned to his apartment with a 12-pack of beer and a few moving boxes. He leaned the boxes on the wall and rested the beer on his knee, against the door, while putting the key in the lock.

Just as Tim was turning the knob, someone inside yanked the door open. The beer slid off Tim's knee and crashed to the floor. One can rolled out of the box and into the apartment with beer spraying out of it. Tim looked up in shock to find Rick standing there grinning at him.

"Sorry dude." Rick said and merely walked passed him as if nothing happened. "Tell her I'll be right back."

"Who... What the fuck? What are you--" Tim watched Rick walk down the hall, then looked back inside the apartment to catch Jill coming out of the kitchen. She stopped when she saw him. The beer can spray continued to splatter lightly against the wall.

Jill said, "You told me I could pick up my things. I thought I'd be out of here before--"

"You're screwing Rick the Dick now?" Tim said as he bent down and grabbed a towel from a laundry basket on the floor and wrapped the leaking can in it.

"No, he's just helping me," Jill said, then paused with a smile that was a little too intrigued for Tim's taste. "Why do you call him that?"

"It's because he's a giant ass and..." Tim looked at her as she softly smiled, wanting more. "Okay, yeah and he hit the fucking genetic lottery with his mutant circus freak-sized cock. Is that what you want to hear?"

"No, I wasn't…"

"You really give the term size-queen new meaning--" Tim stopped abruptly when he spotted a package on the coffee table. His eyes lit up, he walked over to the package and grabbed it.

"That was outside. Look, can we talk about this? It wasn't all about the sex," Jill pleaded.

Tim completely ignored her as he studied the box.

"Tim, I'm really sorry," she continued.

"The sex, it was fine," Tim said, still eyeing the box.

Jill gave him a strange look and watched as he carried the box to the kitchen while trying to open it and she said, "I got all my stuff, but I left you all the DVDs that we--"

Tim called back from the kitchen, "Don't worry about it."

She stared at the doorway where he disappeared and called after him, "Tim?"

"Sure, take the DVDs. You two kids have fun tonight," he yelled back from the other room.

Jill walked into the kitchen and found him holding a pill bottle. When she entered he shoved it back into the box and looked at her with an odd smile.

"Are you okay?" she said.

"Uh, yeah. I'm fine. I'm cool with everything. Really. But do you think you could finish up another time?"

"I'm done. Rick just took out the last box." She looked at him as he held the box, smiling at her with a wide-eyed, nervous expression. "Are you sure?" she asked.

He gave her a quick nod.

"Well, okay then," she said and gave him an odd look as she turned to go.

Once they were out of his hair, Tim stripped down to his white boxer briefs and searched the refrigerator. He contemplated grabbing a beer, paused for a moment then put it back and pulled out a sports drink, thinking that it might be a better choice for his workout. He made his way to the sofa and took a seat. The sports drink and his newly-arrived MaxiManhood pill bottle, along with the ProHairCal and HydroDragenX bottles, sat on the table in front of him.

He slipped on a pair of workout gloves; the freaky looking ones with the fingers cut out. The AutoXerSizer sat next to him. He connected the small pads running out of the device to his chest, biceps, stomach and thighs. He opened up each pill bottle and shook out a pill into his hand. He swallowed the three pills with half the sports drink and placed the drink back on the table.

Tim reached to turn on the device then paused, looking at the pads on his thighs, and an idea hit him. The AutoXerSizer supposedly simulated growth and also brought blood to areas where it was attached. So why not connect it to the area where blood and growth were desperately needed? It seemed like a brilliant idea and what harm could it possibly do? Tim peeled the pads off his thighs and re-attached both of them directly to his penis. He eyed the strange sight for a moment then raised his eyebrows with a confident grin.

He turned on the device and it began to softly hum. He turned the dial from one to five and the humming increased as his body gently shook and it felt pretty good, especially down there. He took a peek in his underwear and smiled. His penis appeared to be already increasing in size. A slight change maybe, but at least it was something. He looked at the dial on the AutoXerSizer and contemplated turning the dial to a higher setting. He had never gone above a seven and that was a little rough, even without it being connected up to his most sensitive of areas. Tim reached for the dial then paused and began an internal mantra of random motivational thoughts like 'desperate times call for desperate measures,' 'no pain no gain' and then he tossed in a 'you only live once.' He continued with his internal deliberations, closing with 'what's the worst that could happen?' He was positive he could pull the pads off quickly if needed. He took a deep breath, then cranked the dial up to ten with one quick spin. The humming grew louder as Tim's entire body trembled. He glanced over to the device and noticed it was beginning to smoke. He reached for it, but was unable to control his arms, which were shaking.

Maybe it was because his thighs had not been connected to the demon-like device that he still had some limited control of his legs, but whatever it was, his thighs seemed to be the only part of his body that he still was able to direct. He stiffened his legs and awkwardly slid down off the sofa to the floor as his upper body continued to shudder. He attempted to reach for the smoking device once more as the humming continued and the lights began to dim in the room. A loud pop was followed by a last violent spasm through his body then he passed out cold and the room went black as the electricity in his and the six other apartments in his wing went out.

twelve - It looked kinda like a crude penis suicide bomb

The next morning the blazing sun shown through the window onto Tim's face and he began to stir. He was still connected to the AutoXerSizer, and was resting in an awkward position with one leg under the coffee table. The wires running to the device were all crossed and tangled around his upper body and neck. He opened his eyes, was overcome by a blast of sunlight, and reflexively tried to shield his face with his hands, but ended up pulling the wires around his neck tighter and the device to the floor. It fell off the table and landed next to his head.

He studied the box, which was now blackened with soot near the vent openings in the back. The wires that ran from it had turned a horrible black color. The wires returned to their normal color about a foot away from the device. He figured the burning had stopped at that point, and he was relieved that it had. Tim slowly pulled himself onto the sofa and scanned his body. He felt a little groggy and sore, but he was not bleeding or injured in any way that he could tell.

He pulled the pads off his body, starting with his arms, then he removed them from his chest and stomach. He noticed red marks where the pads had been. The areas looked to be slightly burned and he rubbed them gently with his fingers. His eyes followed the remaining set of wires, which led into his underwear. A feeling of panic came over him as he looked at his boxer shorts. The pads that were still connected to his penis had left a pair of nearly identical burn marks on his otherwise perfectly white underwear.

Without looking, he cautiously slid his hands into his boxers for a quick check and exhaled deeply when everything felt more or less as he had last remembered it. He slid his boxers down and the inside of his shorts looked kinda like a crude penis suicide bomb. He tested the connection of one of the pads by tugging on it a little and when he found it stuck really well, he pulled his hands back and prepared for the worst. With defusion-like precision, he carefully went back to work on the area, moving wires out of the way, and slowly pulling the pads off one at a time, grimacing as he felt and heard the sound of tearing flesh.

After he had successfully freed his penis from the pads, he leaned back on the sofa, out of breath and with his eyes watering. Tim leaned in and wiped away the tears as he struggled to get a clear look at his manhood. When he was finally able to focus on it, he felt initially relieved that the only disfigurement from his little experiment was the two painful pad-shaped burn marks on either side of the shaft. He touched the discolored areas cautiously and felt some pain, but nothing serious enough to require medical attention. He imagined how he might have explained those marks on his penis at the hospital and began to smile as he went over the possibilities in his mind.

The smile quickly faded and turned to a look of disappointment with the realization that his dick was, in fact, exactly as it had been before. It was still the same pathetic little joke and he was convinced, now more than ever, that he could do nothing to change that.

Tim slumped back into the sofa and pulled his cell phone up to his face to check the time. It was 10:32 AM. He could not believe he had slept ten hours straight. He rubbed his face and then looked at the packing boxes all around him. It was moving day and he jumped up with the realization that Carter would be arriving soon to help.

About an hour later, outside his building, Tim struggled to lift a box into the moving truck. He lost his balance, slammed his groin into the back bumper, and grimaced in excruciating pain. He pushed the box into the truck, closed his eyes, rubbed the affected area and felt something strange. When he looked down at his groin, his eyes widened; the bulge in his shorts was unusually large. He began squeezing all around the area and a broad smile lit up his face. Tim didn't notice that a young girl, about ten years old, and her father were standing there watching him with a look of unspeakable horror on both their faces. He continued grinning and grasped the waistband of his shorts for a better look inside, but stopped when he heard the father gasp. He looked up and saw the father yank his daughter close to him. Tim quickly pulled his hands away from his shorts and said, "Sorry," with a strange glowing smile on his face. The father grabbed the girl's hand and rushed her away.

Tim ran into the apartment building, through the open front door, the living room, bedroom and into the bathroom, where he ripped down his shorts and underwear and stood a few feet back from the mirror, gazing into it at his brand new semi-spectacular penis. His new friend was not only longer, but also thicker, and he looked at it proudly.

He grabbed it with one hand; it felt like it had some real weight to it now. He lifted it up and pulled on it to check it out in the mirror from all angles. Then he looked down directly at it, but his shirt was blocking his view. He quickly lost the shirt and stood again looking in the mirror to take it all in.

Tim stood there naked except for his shoes and socks and started stroking it so he could get the full effect. He quickly pumped it up to a raging hard-on then stood sideways and checked it out in the mirror. He grabbed it with one hand against his body and was pleasantly shocked to find there was still a bunch more of the shaft sticking out from his meaty grip. With the old him, there wasn't much more than the head sticking out after he got a good hold on it, but today there was more of it; a lot more.

He wrapped his other hand around it in a good old-fashioned two-handed backhand tennis grip, and he could still see the very tip of the head. Tim was overjoyed with this transformation and just stared at it. His eyes lit up, then he ran to the bedroom awkwardly, sporting his fairly substantial erection.

Inside the room was a bed with no sheets and a few other pieces of furniture. Some small packing boxes were scattered around the room, and also one large box about four feet high, which sat near the dresser. Tim pondered which box to choose, decided on the large one, and proceeded to search it. He bent over the box and tossed items out behind him in a desperate search.

Finally, Tim said loudly, "There you are," and pulled his trusty wooden ruler out of the box.

As he turned around, Tim was face to face with a groaning Carter. "Ugh." Carter quickly covered his eyes with his hand. When he let his hands down, Tim was still standing there, his half-erect penis dangling between his legs.

"Holy shit. Dude, I didn't know you were a grower."

"Sorry," Tim said, smiling as he rushed back to the bathroom without any attempt to cover himself.

"Dude, are you--" is all Carter could say, as he turned away, horrified.

"Just give me a minute," Tim shouted from the bathroom.

When Tim was fully dressed, he sprinted into the living room, unusually upbeat. Carter sat on the edge of the sofa, holding the fried AutoXerSizer box in his lap. He traced one of the wires from the pad to the device, giving a close look to the soot covered area of wire as it neared the device.

Carter narrowed his eyes, held the device out to Tim and said, "What the fuck is this?" Then he pointed to the charred underwear on the table. "And these and what the--"

Tim ignored all the questions and said, "Dude, you've got to see this."

"I really don't want to see your dick," Carter said recoiling.

"No, not that. My hair. It's growing."

"I, uh, hate to admit noticing, but isn't something else...growing?"

thirteen - The surveillance

While Tim was bringing Carter up to speed, two police officers were stationed in an abandoned house across from the suspicious white house in Tim's parent's neighborhood. They were assigned surveillance duty on the very same white house that the neighbors had all reported to the police, but believed that nothing was being done about. The department had been investigating for a number of months and was close to breaking the case wide open. The surveillance was supposed to provide the break that they needed. Both officers were in their mid-thirties. Officer Sam White stood looking out the window with binoculars, while Officer Larry Martin sat behind him, sleepily reviewing documents.

Coming into Sam's view were Tim and Carter in a moving truck. Sam said, "It's that Garrett boy in a moving truck. Looks like he's moving back home and he has some help with him."

Larry looked at Sam and perked up just a little. "Tell me it's a hot girlfriend?"

"No, just some guy."

Larry rolled his eyes and returned back to the documents, disinterested. Then Larry looked back to Sam and added, "You don't think that's his boyfriend do you?"

"No," said Sam as he continued to watch the truck. Then he lowered the binoculars and looked back at Larry. "Well, maybe."

"Because I can't take another sausage-fest surveillance next to a gay couple. They are always showing off how amazing their sex lives are. They leave the blinds up, the lights on and they're constantly doing it. Just once I would like a nice horny couple where the woman is incredibly hot. Is that too much to ask for with one of these boring ass assignments?"

"You mean that last couple with the combined weight of five hundred pounds didn't do it for you?"

Larry gave Sam a sickened look and said, "I was trying to forget about them. Shit, did you--"

"Remember how much pubic hair she had?"

"I do now," Larry said scowling.

Sam grinned at Larry, then looked back out the window at the truck and swung back to the white house just as a man in his late fifties emerged from it. The man walked down the driveway and into the street and Sam said, "I think he's going for it."

Sam shifted the binoculars for a view of a vacant house where a package sat on the porch as Larry got up and stood behind him. As the man approached the vacant house, Larry said, "We've got him."

As the man neared the driveway, Sam said "Come on. Take it old man." But despite all the encouragement, the man walked past the house and kept going. Larry walked back to his chair as Sam looked at him and said, "Shit. We've been watching that fucking package for almost two days and no one has come near it. I've got to get out of here. I'm losing it."

At Tim's house, Carter and Tim took a break after unloading half the truck. They left most of his stuff in the garage since Tim's parents had pretty much told him not to make himself too comfortable. Luckily, they would be gone for two weeks, which would give Tim time to recover from the whole Jill situation and possibly find other living arrangements. He figured if he wasn't up to moving out by the time they got back, it would probably be okay with them. At least he kept telling himself that.

Carter and Tim stood outside his old bedroom, staring at the key-locked door. Tim said, "How could they do this to my room?"

"This is a pretty heavy duty lock," Carter said.

"You think they're trying to send me a message? "

"Yeah, the message is keep the fuck out of here," Carter said, chuckling.

Tim shrugged then tried the doorknob unsuccessfully. "Screw this."

When they finished unloading the truck, Tim brought it back to the rental place and returned home in his car. In the kitchen, he looked out to the backyard to find Carter floating in the pool, beer in hand. Tim reached into a box on the counter and pulled out the three pill bottles. He swallowed his hair growth, fat reduction and magic cock pills with a swig of water. Then he grabbed the bulge in his pants for a quick check and acknowledged that it was still unusually healthy.

Tim walked out to the backyard and approached Carter in the pool and said, "Come on let's go."

Carter said, "This place is amazing. We've got to bring some girls back here tonight. You get some girls a little drunk from the bar who don't happen to have their bathing suits handy and one thing leads to another and they're swimming in just a bra and panties. Then maybe the bra comes off and... You ever bang any chicks in this pool?"

"No, my parents were always home."

"Well, now's your chance."

fourteen - Just tell her you've got this brand new big dick and ask her if she wants to be the first one to try it out

Later at MacGrubey's Pub, Tim and Carter stood near the bar drinking beer. They exchanged glances with two attractive young women from across the room then looked at one another. Tim said, "What should I say?"

"Just tell her you've got this brand new big dick and ask her if she wants to be the first one to try it out."

"There's something seriously wrong with you," Tim said, scowling at him.

"Okay, then do what the old pathetic loser you would do. Just stand here."

"Screw that, let's go over," Tim said and the pair walked over to the girls. Tim had his eye on Jessica, the hot athletic-looking brunette. He stood drinking and talking with her and doing quite well as Carter struggled with Jessica's friend, who appeared as though she'd prefer to be almost anywhere else on the planet.

Tim and Jessica made their way to the bar for another round. While waiting for the bartender, Tim said something that cracked her up then she lost her balance and fell against him, accidentally making contact with his groin. She pulled back and looked down at it, then up to his face. He smiled and whispered into her ear that it was way too hot in the bar, that he had a pool back at his place and would she like to come back with him and cool off.

Jessica nodded and they stared into each other's eyes, a little drunk and a lot horny. Jessica headed over to speak to her friend and Tim waved off the bartender. Then Tim followed her, eyes glued on her gorgeous ass as he struggled to believe his luck.

When they reached their friends, Tim and Jessica proposed going back to Tim's place for a swim. Carter nodded eagerly while the girl twisted her mouth in evident dissatisfaction. Jessica pulled her friend aside and they spoke briefly, but the girl didn't try to hide her dislike for Carter, and after looking him over once more, she shook her head at Jessica and walked away. Jessica walked over to Tim and the pair gave Carter a sorrowful shrug, then quickly headed for the door.

Back at the abandoned house, Larry and Sam continued their surveillance. Larry looked out the window with binoculars at the package, which still remained on the porch of the vacant house. He followed the two cars that drove into his field of view as they pulled into the Garrett driveway. Tim and Jessica got out of their cars and headed for the house. Tim carried a bag containing his overpriced convenience store 3-pack of Magnums. Larry said to Sam, "Our new friend has a date."

Sam rushed over with binoculars to check it out. They both watched as a light came on in the Garrett house living room and Tim and Jessica stumbled into the room kissing, clearly visible through the large bay window. The officers continued to watch as the horny pair hungrily struggled to remove each other's clothes.

"Shit, she's hot," said Sam.

"I'll bet you she has those little pink nipples," said Larry.

"I'm going with medium-sized brown ones."

Sam and Larry took a break from the scene to look at one another and Larry asked, "Ten bucks?"

"Make it twenty."

"You're on," said Larry and they both returned to the Garrett house window as Jessica reached to unclasp her bra with Tim, Sam and Larry all waiting slack-jawed. While Sam and Larry were impatiently waiting for the nipple unveiling, a man approached the porch of the vacant house undetected by the otherwise occupied officers.

After Jessica removed her bra, Sam and Larry focused in on her beautiful breasts and she did in fact have tiny little pink nipples, enriching Larry and disappointing Sam.

Tim and Jessica stood a few feet apart. Jessica removed her mini skirt and stood wearing nothing but panties as Tim removed everything except his boxer shorts. She pushed her panties down off her waist then shimmied her hips until they slid to the floor. She stepped out of the underwear with one foot, sent her underwear flying a few feet away, and eyed Tim expectantly. Tim looked her over eagerly, exhaled deeply, then dropped his underwear quickly, with virtually no shimmying whatsoever. Jessica glanced down to his large penis and her jaw dropped.

As both officers remained glued to the scene, on the porch of the vacant house the man grabbed the package and slipped away.

"What the... Is that real?" said Larry.

"Fucking lucky bastard," said Sam.

Sam and Larry looked at one another, shocked, then returned to the window as Jessica kissed her way down Tim's body to rest on her knees. Jessica held Tim's penis in her hands and it continued to grow. She licked her lips and contemplated the large equipment.

Larry said, "There's no way."

Sam said, "How is she going to-" just as Jessica somehow put about half of it in her mouth and all Sam could say was, "Oh, okay."

"She's really talented," said Larry, and by the look on Tim's face he was also in agreement.

Jessica pulled back and looked it over again in deep admiration. Then she reached up and pulled Tim to the floor and out of sight of the officer voyeurs.

"Fuck," said Larry as he and Sam shared a look. "Let me know if she comes back up for air."

Larry walked away while Sam looked casually out the window back toward the vacant house. When he could not spot the package, he frantically scanned all around the front of the house then yelled, "Shit!"

"What?"

"The package is gone."

Larry rushed back, looked out the window scanning all around the vacant house, then dropped the binoculars on the floor and glared at Sam.

Back inside the Garrett house, Tim watched as Jessica enthusiastically returned to pleasing him. He could not believe how big he was and wasn't sure if he was more impressed with his current size, or with how she was doing what she was doing. One thing he was sure of was that it was now bigger than it had been when he checked it earlier. He thanked the MaxiManhood Laboratories people over and over while trying to focus on anything other than having an orgasm and prematurely ending this incredible event. This was the first time a girl had given him head and actually genuinely been into it; really, really, into it. In fact, it put the previously, thought to be awesome, Jillian Taylor lobster-induced blowjob to shame.

After a few more intense minutes, Jessica pulled away from him, crawled up and knelt cowgirl style with her target area hovering mere microns over his giant erection. He stammered, "I, uh… Let me get a condom."

"I'll do it," she said and she climbed off him and retrieved the Magnums. He watched her as she opened the box, removed one from the pack, opened it and skillfully slipped it on him as if she had a lot of experience in that area.

Jessica returned to her hovering position, grabbed his penis with one hand and put her other hand on his chest to steady herself. Tim had always been leery of the girl on top positions. He had seen the porn movies where the girls were violently bouncing up and down on those tree-trunk-sized porn guys, and the ones where the guy would be flipping and tossing the girl around effortlessly while he was still inside her, and he was always amazed. His old, thin penis would bend, get knocked around and feel like it could snap in half at any second when a girl started to get rough, and he would cringe and switch to a safer position. But his new thick penis was really holding its own, and it was if that bad boy could hold her up all by itself.

Jessica closed her eyes tightly and her mouth opened wide as she was clearly feeling all of him. This was the reaction he was hoping for, and it was a long way away from the 'Is it in yet?' look that he had up until this moment been so accustomed to.

Jessica looked him in the eye and said, "Let's go slow, okay?"

"Yeah, sure."

She closed her eyes, held her breath and slid slowly down and down and down on him. It seemed like forever, but was actually about fifteen seconds until he was all the way in. She looked at him, exhaled deeply and said, "God, you've got one great fucking cock."

That was just about the most perfect thing that a woman could say in this particular situation and Tim beamed. "Uh, thanks. It's new-- I mean..."

She gave him a strange look, and Tim looked away a little embarrassed. Thankfully, she let it go. She started slowly riding him with her eyes rolling back in her head. She moved faster and faster with her breathing more labored until she exploded in a huge screaming orgasm. This was the first orgasm he'd ever delivered hands-free, and pride exuded from his face. She fell on top of him in a heap of exhaustion, turned her head to him and in heavy breath whispered, "That was wonderful! What can I... What do you want me to do to you? I'll do anything."

"Anything?"

fifteen - Who measures it after the age of sixteen?

Larry slept as Sam kept watch out the window with binoculars. The sun had risen and it was a beautiful day. He scanned over to the inactive white house, then to the vacant house, and when he heard a car start, he looked over to the Garrett house and watched as Jessica drove down the driveway and into the street. After she was gone, Sam looked into the Garrett house to find Tim naked from the waist down carrying a magazine and a ruler. Sam said loudly, "You prick," which knocked Larry out of his deep sleep.

Larry bolted upright, looked at him and said, "What the hell are you doing?"

"You've got to see this," Sam said as Tim disappeared behind a wall and out of his view then he added, "Wait. Shit." Seconds later Tim came back into view and sat down on the sofa. "Okay, yeah. Look at this arrogant douche bag."

Larry came over, binoculars in hand, and looked out the window. The pair had a clear view of Tim as he began leafing through the magazine with one hand and getting himself aroused with the other. Larry said, "Jesus, I don't need to see this. Can we arrest this asshole for something?"

Tim looked down at his dick proudly and then grabbed the ruler, prompting Sam and Larry to look away. Sam said, "Who measures it after the age of sixteen?"

Larry gave him a tired look and said, "Can we get reassigned?"

After the measurement, Tim was even happier than he was when Jessica was using him in that pommel horse like fashion. He skipped gleefully upstairs to the bathroom where he stood at the mirror and swallowed the three pills. He leaned in close to study the hair growing on his head. He removed his shirt, flexed his muscles. He was starting to see some more definition there, as well. He looked down at his penis proudly.

Later that day, Tim went to the mall to purchase more accommodating underwear. As he walked out of a store, he discovered Rachael sitting on a bench near a children's play area. He approached her and said, "Hey you."

She smiled up at him, keeping one eye on the play area and said, "Tim, hey how are you?"

"I heard about the email thing. I can't believe they just fired you like that. I'm so sorry."

"It was crazy. I couldn't even go back to my desk. They escorted me out."

"But you were going to delete that email."

"I did. At least I thought I did. It was still in my drafts folder. I don't know. Somehow I must have sent it... and the customer sent it to Beverly. It was a nightmare," Rachael said with a frown.

"Is there anything I can do?"

Rachael shook her head no and looked around him, distracted, to the play area. He stepped aside and followed her gaze and asked, "What are you doing here?"

"I'm here with my kids," Rachael said. She perked back up as she watched her children, a boy and a girl who looked to be close in age, around five or six, enjoying the slide in the play area.

"You have kids?" Tim said, a bit thrown.

She looked at him, a little annoyed, and he tried to recover by saying, "No, I mean you just don't look like...You're so young."

"And stupid. It's a long story, but I wouldn't change a thing. They're my life," Rachael said, smiling as the kids returned and sat next to her.

"Can we get ice cream now?" David asked.

Rachael smiled at him and said, "Sure we can." Then she looked at Tim, "Tim this is David and Clare. Kids, this is Mr. Tim."

Tim smiled at the kids and they waved, then began grabbing books from their mother's bag. Rachael watched them proudly.

She looked back to Tim, "You were moving, weren't you? Did you ever find a place?"

Tim paused then tried to come up with a story that didn't make him sound lame, but stammered instead, "Not really, I moved back... I'm actually house-sitting, for a couple, temporarily. The place has a pool. You guys should come over some time. The kids could swim. I could cook."

"I always wanted a pool growing up," she said.

The kids looked up from their books, excited. David said, "I want to swim mommy."

Clare chimed in with, "Can we swim today?"

Rachael looked at the kids as if they had done something wrong, and they delivered back sad faces. Rachael said, "I'm sure Mr. Tim is busy today."

"No, not really," Tim replied.

Rachael looked at him apologetically and he simply smiled at her and said, "Really, it's okay. Why don't you come over in a couple of hours? I'll make something for dinner."

The kids looked at Rachael and pleaded to go. This broke her heart and she looked back up to Tim again. "Are you sure?"

sixteen - This one has a hole in it. A big hole

Tim was preparing food in the kitchen when the doorbell rang. He walked to the front door, opened it and Rachael's kids rushed past him to the back of the house. Tim grinned and shook his head as he turned to watch, then he looked back to Rachael and said, "You found it okay?"

"Your directions were great." Rachael tried to look around Tim with concern over what the kids might be doing. "Oh God, I hope--"

Tim gave her a comforting look and said, "Don't worry about them. I did a little child proofing." He reached out to take the beach bag from her.

David yelled from somewhere within the house, "Mommy."

"Mommy, come see the pretty pool," Clare said.

"They're a little excited," Rachael explained as she stepped into the foyer.

When Tim and Rachael made their way to the great room, they found the kids standing mesmerized in front of a fish tank. "Mommy look, lobsters," Clare said.

Rachael eyed the tank strangely, "Wow, you don't normally see people raising their own, uh, lobsters."

"No, they're pets. Kind of," Tim said and she gave him a curious look. After a brief awkward moment he felt the need to elaborate, "Originally they were going to be dinner. But they stuck with me during a rough patch, so..."

Rachael humored him with half a smile.

Later, out by the pool, the kids swam and Rachael sat on the edge of the pool in a bikini as Tim worked the grill. Tim gazed at her as she watched the kids and her body looked amazing by any standard, but especially for a woman with two children. He wondered if it bothered him that she had kids, but after one look at her in that bikini, he didn't care how many kids she had.

She smiled up at him and he quickly lifted his eyes off her cleavage and up to her face and said, "I wasn't sure what they liked so I made hamburgers, hot dogs, and barbecue chicken. Oh, and I bought some of those frozen chicken nugget things."

Impressed, Rachael looked at him and said, "You really shouldn't have gone to all that trouble, but it sounds great."

"I think there are some floats over in the box next to the house. Have them pick something out and I'll blow it up."

After Clare made her selection, Rachael walked over to Tim at the grill and said, "I'll take over while you blow it up."

Tim connected the air compressor nozzle to the float and plugged the power cord into the outlet. The float quickly started to expand as he stood holding it in front of Clare, who waited patiently. As the float took shape, Tim noticed something unusual about it.

As Clare said, "It's a pretty lady," he noticed that although the float was rectangular, just like a traditional raft, it had a life-sized, anatomically correct image of a naked woman on the front, along with a hole right where the actual female genital hole would be. He moved his hand down to the area just to be sure it was actually a hole and when his fingers slid all the way inside it, he began to panic. Was this a freaking love doll float? Where would someone even purchase something like that? Was it possible that his parents actually owned such an obscene float? No, there was no way. They didn't actually have sex anymore, did they? He was sure they hadn't in at least ten years.

He yanked the power cord out of the outlet and attempted to fold up the pornographic float so the kids and Rachael would not get a look at it. Since it was already mostly full of air, it was difficult to conceal. When Clare reached to grab it, he pulled it away and quickly said, "Clare honey, this one has a hole in it. A big hole. Could you pick something else?"

Rachael looked over at the commotion as a gust of wind caught the float and turned the naked lady side in her direction, giving her a shocking glimpse. Tim saw Rachael's expression change, and he swiftly dropped the float to the concrete and pounced on top of it, knees first. When it popped, Rachael gave him a concerned look.

Tim glanced up to her apologetically and said, "Sorry, I, uh, remember I'm just house-sitting." He pushed the remaining air out of the float and carefully rolled it up. He stood, grabbed Clare by the hand and walked her to the pool box. While Clare was busy searching, he quickly glanced to confirm Rachael was not looking his way and then discreetly tossed the naked lady pool float behind him and over the fence.

Later they all sat on the patio at the table eating. Clare looked up to Tim and said sweetly, "Can I have my birthday party here?"

Rachael said, "Clare, you can't ask Mr. Tim to--"

"How old are you going to be?" Tim said, amused by her candor.

"Six."

"When's your birthday?"

"Saturday."

Tim smiled at Rachael, who was shaking her head in disbelief, then he looked back to Clare. "Sure, you can have your party here."

"We couldn't. We're just having a few of her friends over the apartment," said Rachael.

Clare said, "Mommy, I really want a swim party."

"Clare, I'm sure Mr. Tim has other plans."

"Actually, I don't," Tim admitted.

After the meal and more swimming, Tim was in the kitchen loading the dishwasher as the kids watched TV in the great room. Rachael walked into the room wearing Tim's shorts and one of his t-shirts. Her hair was slicked back and she looked fantastic. Tim glanced at her chest briefly and was glad he had offered her that white shirt, since he could pretty clearly see a hint of nipples and deduced that she must be braless. Tim closed the dishwasher as Rachael leaned against the counter near him.

"I can't believe I forgot to bring a change of clothes," she said.

"No problem," Tim answered, and then he looked around for the kids. "It's too quiet. What happened?"

"They're wiped out. About the party, I'll make up something to save you."

"What are you talking about?"

"If you're house-sitting, do you really think you should be hosting a kid's birthday party?"

Tim looked at her as he prepared to come clean, paused and said, "That couple. They're actually my... parents."

"Oh, so you crawled back home," she said smiling. "But still..."

"It's not a big deal and if it means I get to spend some time with you then..."

She looked at him, still not certain until he returned a convincing shrug that won her over. "Okay," Rachael conceded. "But you won't have to do a thing. I'll come early, decorate and take care of the food and everything."

Later, Tim and Rachael sat outside near the pool on lounge chairs and watched the kids sleeping in the great room through the window. Tim listened attentively as Rachael opened up and told her life's story. She became pregnant the very first time she had sex, with her very first real boyfriend, at the age of eighteen. To make matters worse, the site of her deflowering was, of all places, on top of her father's prized pool table in the basement of the family's home. Rachael blushed as she admitted that the pool table was still there, along with the never identified tiny discoloration on the green felt from her ill-timed coupling. Whenever she was at home, the sight of it reminded her of what brought her to this place in her life.

She and her boyfriend decided to keep the baby and get married, and a few months after the first one, a second child was on the way. The second one was more her fault. Rachael had rolled over onto her wonderful new husband in the middle of one sleep deprived night and one thing led to another, no protection was used, and that was that. The marriage had always been a little rocky, she admitted.

"Wow. I had no idea you've been through all this," Tim said softly.

She took a sip of her drink and continued her story. "Then two years ago, he decided he didn't want to be married anymore."

"So, you're divorced?"

"No, we're only separated. He won't sign the papers."

Tim tried to hide his disappointment. "Does he want to get back together?"

"He claims he's changed, but I'm not convinced. I don't want to talk about him." Rachael shook her head and looked through the window at her children.

Tim watched her closely, studying her as the light from the window spilled across her face. He replayed that last day at work with her in his mind, and how he screwed it up.

Rachael turned toward him. "What is it?"

"I, uh… That day at work. I'm sorry I didn't take you up on your lunch offer."

"I know. What was up with that?" she said grinning as she put her drink on the table between them, and then swung her legs off the lounge chair and onto the patio to face him.

"I'm a moron," he admitted.

She leaned a little closer to him with a soft smile and as he looked into her eyes she whispered, "You were." Rachael moved her lips to his slowly and kissed him. He was surprised at first, but then returned the kiss. She placed a hand on his chest and kissed him more passionately, then they slowly pulled away from each other. See looked back at the kids then smiled at him. "It's late and I should get them home. But I'll see you next week."

He nodded, then she leaned in and kissed him on the cheek. She looked like she might want to cry. "Are you okay?" Tim asked with concern. "What is it?"

"Nothing. This was really nice. The kids haven't had this much fun in a long time." She pulled herself together a little and smiled at him. They started walking toward the door.

seventeen - The Theodore Garrett Signature Replica Penis

In the den, Tim struggled to sleep on the horribly uncomfortable pullout sofa. (As if there were any other kind.) He grabbed his phone off the table and checked the time, which showed 1:34 AM. He rolled over, adjusted the pillow and tried to clear his mind, but that damn bar was sticking right into his back through that piece of shit thin mattress. He threw a mini temper tantrum, thrashed on the bed and punched the thin crappy mattress. He unfortunately struck the mattress just over the deadly bar, which caused him to grasp his hand in agony and let off a string of intense profanity. Tim sat up as his hand continued to throb and decided he had the perfect solution for both his hand and his inability to sleep; he would drink himself to pain-free unconsciousness.

After three beers, Tim returned to the horrible sofa bed with a slight buzz and drifted off to sleep briefly before being jarred awake again by the bar stabbing into his back. He grabbed his phone and checked the time, which now showed 2:42 AM. He sat up, tossed his phone onto the bed and threw off the covers.

Back in the kitchen, Tim grabbed another beer and a screwdriver from the tool drawer and made his way to his old bedroom door. When he reached the door, he eyed the lock and shook his head in disbelief. He took a long sip of beer, placed the bottle on the floor and went to work on the lock. He pushed hard on the screwdriver, slipped, and jammed his hand into the doorknob. He jumped back, screaming in pain. Frustrated, he punched the door and then leaned against it, exhausted, with his eyes closed. He rested there briefly until a thought came to him.

Tim ran to the kitchen and searched through the drawers collecting old keys. He brought about half a dozen to the door and tried them all without success. He entered his parent's bedroom and stood there thinking. He walked over to a chest of drawers and searched each drawer for keys, but found nothing. He approached the bed, pulled down the comforter, and resigned himself to the possibility that he just might be able to sleep there. He was worn out, mostly buzzed, and he could pretty much sleep in any real bed, even one that his parents had sex in. He found it a little more bearable as he believed it had to have been at least a few years since they had actually done it there. As he tried to remove that image from his brain, he pulled the blanket down to find flaming red satin sheets and stepped back, a little freaked out. He promptly tossed the blanket and comforter back over the bed and turned to look around the room, racking his brain for the next bright idea. He remembered the briefcase his father kept and he headed toward the closet, beer in hand.

He found it exactly where it had always been. The case was where his father kept his adult magazine and porn video stash. Tim had discovered the case when he was around fifteen and found it locked, but even back then it only took him a few tries to deduce the combination. He proceeded to spend the better part of his high school years sneaking into the closet, whenever he found himself alone in the house, so he could enjoy his father's collection. After each viewing, Tim made sure to put everything back exactly as he had found it, and he was almost positive his father never knew. Now he figured the case would be a perfect place to hide the key to his old bedroom.

The case sat on a shelf about eight feet off the floor and just out of his reach. For a moment, Tim considered getting a chair, but then realized that the only chairs were downstairs and in his mildly inebriated state, he might just take a tumble down the stairs and break his neck while hauling it up. Rather than put down the beer, he held it in one hand while he stood on his tiptoes and found he could reach the outside edge of the handle. He struggled, stretched further and with one last open-mouthed reach, he was finally able to grasp the handle. When he pulled the handle down, it caused the back of the case to lean up.

On top of the case and out of his view were some items and papers, which began sliding toward his face. A small, flesh-colored dildo rolled off the top and directly into his still-open mouth. A large clear plastic tube followed the dildo, and nailed him right in the head. With all the crap hitting him in the head and with the surprise visitor in his mouth, Tim lost his balance. He might have been able to steady himself if it hadn't been for the beer he was stupidly holding in his other hand. Instead, he fell backward, knocking clothes off hangers and he landed on the floor smacking his head onto a small fire safe in the process. He lay there, out cold, with the beer spilling onto his chest and the dildo still halfway lodged in his mouth.

Carter arrived the next morning for their planned tennis match and found Tim's car in the driveway, but when he rang the doorbell repeatedly, there was no answer. Carter walked to the backyard and relaxed in a chair by the pool. After a few minutes, he knocked on the patio door and found it unlocked, so he let himself in.

After unsuccessfully calling for and searching for Tim downstairs, he proceeded upstairs. When he entered the master bedroom, he noticed the closet door open with a body lying inside and he rushed over to investigate. When he entered the closet, he was shocked to find Tim on the ground with what looked like some sort of fake penis lying a half-inch from his open mouth. Next to that was an instruction page for the 'Copy-a-Cock – Make a Replica of Any Penis' kit.

Carter leaned down and made sure that Tim was still breathing. He picked up the instructions and looked them over, horrified, as they graphically depicted how one might make an exact replica of their penis using the kit. He tried to match up all the items from the kit depicted in the instructions with the items that were scattered on the floor. He looked at the molding tube, which lay next to Tim, and then he watched as Tim began to stir. Tim rolled slightly toward the dildo and wrapped his hands around a pile of clothes that were near his head. The dildo got caught up in the clothes and as Tim pulled the pillow-like pile closer to his head the dildo slid into his open mouth. Carter watched and shook his head in disgust.

Tim, still asleep, began to look uncomfortable with the foreign object jammed in his mouth, but it wasn't until he cuddled with the clothes pile a little tighter that it slipped in too far and began to choke him. Tim rolled over so he was face up, choking, with the dildo now lodged halfway down his throat. His eyes quickly opened and he stared back at Carter in shock. Tim grabbed the object from his mouth and pulled it out. He sat up and eyed it strangely as he struggled to focus. When he finally realized what it was, he threw it to the floor as Carter gave him a sickened look.

"Dude, I can't believe that you made a replica of your own dick. What the fuck is wrong with you?" Carter said.

"What are you taking about?"

"And why were you practicing giving it a blowjob?"

Tim looked at him in a daze. "What, what replica?"

"The Copy-a-Cock kit."

Tim gave him a confused stare and Carter handed over the instruction sheet. Tim reviewed the sheet and then picked up the dildo. When he turned it over, he noticed some writing etched into the flat bottom base.

Tim read it and instantly collapsed onto the floor, curled up in fetal position and gurgled like he had been poisoned. "Please find something and kill me. I can't--"

Carter picked up the dildo and read the writing out loud, breaking into laughter halfway through. "Connie, Happy Anniversary, my penis belongs to you, Ted." When he was finally able to stop laughing, Carter gave him a horrified look. "Okay, so why are you practicing giving a blowjob to the Theodore Garrett Signature Replica Penis?"

Tim glared at him then turned a strange pale green color and said, "Oh shit, I think I'm going to be sick." He began coughing violently, stood up and ran past Carter into the bathroom. He knelt at the toilet, wrapped his hands around it and dry heaved into the bowl. He wiped his mouth, stood, slowly made his way to the sink and frantically searched the cabinets until he found mouthwash. As he gargled with tears streaming down his face, Carter entered the bathroom holding the dildo. Carter held it out to him waiting for an explanation. Tim looked at him, coughed again then after a few seconds struggled to explain.

"I wasn't-- I couldn't sleep on that damn pullout piece of shit, so I was trying to find the key to my old bedroom and when I pulled down that briefcase all this crap fell on me. I must have hit my head and I have no idea how that thing got stuck in my mouth."

Carter looked at him, then looked back at the tiny dildo and said, grinning, "Jesus your dad does have a small dick. Now we know where you…"

Tim glared at him and when Carter tried to hand him the replica, Tim refused it and said, "I'm not touching that thing. Get it away from me. I think I'm going to have to kill myself." Tim walked out of the bathroom back toward the closet with Carter following. Tim said, "Help me find the key to my room. There is no way I'm sleeping on that sofa again."

Carter looked at the bed and said, "What about your parent's bed?"

Tim ignored the comment as they entered the closet and he grabbed his head while eyeing the safe on the floor and said, "I think I hit my head on that." He paused for a moment and then he bent over to pick it up. The safe was heavy, but small enough to be carried. The combination lock was a series of four dials, each numbered zero through nine.

Tim placed the safe on the bed and tried a combination. When it didn't work, he tried another, which still did not open the safe. He searched his mind for a moment, then smiled and tried one more combination. He dialed up 0-9-

2-5, September twenty-fifth, his parent's anniversary, and the lock clicked open. He smiled and opened the safe.

Carter moved over for a better look as Tim lifted the lid and removed documents and placed them aside. He grinned when he pulled out a set of door keys and the keys to the BMW.

Tim unlocked and opened the door to his old bedroom. When he turned the light on, he was revolted to find not a Feng Shui retreat, but something along the lines of a sex den. He walked in, mesmerized, and Carter followed with a silly grin on his face.

"Man, your parents are freaks," Carter said.

The room was painted a bright red and the windows were covered by light-blocking shades, for the obvious privacy that a room of this type would demand. In one corner was a black sex swing, which hung from a large hook in the ceiling. A hot pink inflatable cushion with a matching giant pink dildo attachment sat in another corner.

Carter walked over to the sex swing, studied it and said, "I've never seen one of these in person. It looks really uncomfortable."

Tim eyed the pink inflatable and said, "Feng Shui my ass!"

"What?" Carter said as he looked at Tim confused, but Tim just ignored the question and looked like he might be on the verge of having an aneurysm as he took in the rest of his parent's secret room. On the other side of the room were a sex mat, a sex ramp and wedge, assorted sex toys and lotions. Tim said, "This is more like Fuck Shui."

In the corner Tim spotted a massage table. He nodded and said, "Okay, so they didn't lie about the massage." Carter looked at him and he elaborated, "My parents told me this was their massage slash relaxation room."

"You could really relax in here all right."

They both wore rubber kitchen gloves as they loaded all the sex paraphernalia into the already half-full closet in Tim's old room. Tim stood on a chair and removed the sex swing from a hook in the ceiling. Carter folded up the portable massage table and placed it into the closet. Tim shoved the hot pink inflatable cushion and struggled to close the door.

With the room now completely empty, Tim eyed the bold red paint and decided he would just have to live with the color. The pair brought up Tim's bed, dresser and his other belongings and furnished the room. Later that day Tim took his cocktail of pills, checked his hair growth and other growth area, and slept better than he had in weeks.

eighteen - You did that thing. That-- You've had fat injected into it!

On Monday after basketball, Tim, Carter, Rick and the five other sweaty players were undressing in the locker room. Tim stood shirtless in front of his locker and removed his shorts and underwear. Rick glanced at Tim, whose dick had now grown to the point where it was hanging about halfway to his knees. Rick looked again when he noticed the big change, his eyes widened and he smiled broadly. "Holy fuck dude. You're sporting a partial."

All the other guys looked over as Tim looked down at his dick and smiled proudly. Then he looked back up at Rick as the guys started to laugh.

Tim was bigger now in his unaroused state as all the guys, including Rick, were when they were at their rock hard best, and they all knew it.

Rick said, "A partial. Partial wood. I knew you were gay. You can't be in this sausage factory without--"

"It's not. You're the one checking it out, you ass," Tim shot back.

A random black guy entered the locker room from the gym and halted to a stop as he took in the scene. He looked at Tim and glanced down at his groin, and his eyes widened. "I, uh, was just going to take a piss, but..." he announced, then looked back to Tim and said, "Shit. Now

I know what it feels like to be white." Then he turned and walked back out the door.

The group watched the door as it closed and then slowly they returned to the main attraction. Rick snapped out of it first and pointed at Tim laughing. Tim wrapped a towel around himself as he shot back an evil look. Rick paused then grinned, "Wait, I know. I've heard about this. You did that thing. That-- You've had fat injected into it!"

"No. What? Jesus, I..."

The guys chuckled and waited for an answer. Tim stood speechless until Carter offered, "He's taking these pills."

Tim glared at Carter then looked to the guys who waited expectantly. Tim paused then bent down and took his time rummaging around his bag, exaggerating his struggle to locate the white plastic bottle. When seconds past and interest did not falter, Tim reluctantly held up the pills and confessed, "I saw them on TV." He placed the bottle on the shelf of his locker. The guys looked down at themselves then back at Tim, pensively. Tim gave the guys a look like they were freaking him out as he headed to the shower.

One of the basketball players turned to another and said, "Would you ever try something like that?"

"Don't need it."

"Me neither," he said with as much manufactured confidence as he could muster.

nineteen - It's your duty to find them, have sex with them and...

That week, back at work, Tim walked toward the office building behind a group of women, which included Kelly, the one who blew him off at the door just a few days before. This time the women noticed him and Kelly stared at him hungrily while she held the door for him. He walked through, pleasantly surprised, and then headed to the turnstile. The women stood watching him and Kelly whispered something to the group.

Tim scanned his badge then looked back, smiling at the women. Unaware that the turnstile didn't drop, he walked right into it groin first then grabbed the area and struggled to hide the pain. The women looked on concerned as he scanned his badge again, the turnstile dropped, and he walked through with a slight limp.

At lunch in the corporate cafeteria, Tim and Carter sat at a table eating while Kelly and another woman sat on the other side of the room. Carter glanced at them then looked at Tim. "Dude, she wants you."

"She freaking hates me."

"Look at her. She would tear you to pieces, but she definitely wants you."

"How do you know?"

"Kelly told Lisa. Lisa told Barbara who told me."

Tim recalled the door holding incident, smiled and said, "She did hold the door for me this morning."

Carter nodded, but Tim suddenly lost his smile and said, "I want to see what happens with Rachael first. I really think--"

Carter glared at him, "You're an idiot. If I were you, I wouldn't be chasing some girl with kids. I'd be banging every chick I could find. You've been given a gift. You don't need to make small talk anymore, or pretend to be interested in what they're saying, or work for it at all. There are women who will fuck you purely based on this gift. It's your duty to find them, have sex with them and..."

Carter kept going with his passionate speech, but his voice trailed away in Tim's mind as he began to daydream. Let's say hypothetically a guy happens upon a naked woman. She's mildly attractive, but mainly she's naked and she wants to have sex with you. Most guys would stick around, right? And the woman wouldn't really even need to be all that great looking, right? Now switch that around so that a woman happens upon a naked guy and even if he's amazing looking, she's running away screaming, right? But what if that same guy had some monstrous penis? Would the woman be so mesmerized that once she saw it, she would be powerless to resist it? She would have to experience it, wouldn't she? Tim wasn't planning on walking around naked or anything, but he wanted to be that guy. He would continue taking the pills until he got there.

Carter concluded with, "… you know I'm right," just as Kelly stood up, smiled at Tim and headed toward him. Tim turned his head to watch Kelly and they both stared as she approached.

When Kelly reached them, she leaned across the table to Tim, all cleavage, and said, "Tim." There was something about the way she said it. He had never heard his name sound like that before. It was like she had just said, "Tim, I want to suck your cock for like an hour and a half." Tim looked at her a little strangely as he tried to process what was happening, and stammered back with a lame, "Hiya Kelly."

Tim swallowed hard and tried his best to avoid eyeing her chest, then wondered where the hell he came up with "Hiya." Thoughts of beating himself up over his greeting left him as he glanced at her cleavage dreamily, then back to her face when she said, "There's going to be another happy hour on Monday. It's going to be amazing. I'm serious."

"Really. Monday. I've got a bunch of... I'll see if I can make it."

"I hope you can," Kelly said sexily, then she walked away and they watched her open-mouthed.

twenty - The moon bounce

On Saturday, the Garrett backyard was decorated with streamers, balloons and party lights. Tim was able to secure, at a very reasonable price, a full-size moon bounce, which he had the installation crew place right next to the pool. The backyard looked like any kids dream party and it appeared like he might be overdoing it, slightly. Okay, so he was definitely overdoing it.

On the patio, Tim was climbing down a ladder as Rachael walked through the gate carrying a small bag of decorations. She took it all in, astonished, and as she walked slowly to the patio she said, "I thought you weren't going to any trouble."

"I just decorated a little."

Rachael pointed to the moon bounce and said, "And what's this?"

"I know a guy. Really."

She shook her head, feigning disappointment, and held up her tiny bag of decorations." It looks like you won't need these," she said.

He took the bag, looked inside and said unconvincingly, "No, these are great. They'll add to the overall..." He gave her a charming smile.

She grinned at him then looked over the backyard again smiling. "Okay. This looks amazing. My mother is bringing the kids in an hour. I came early to setup, but it looks like you're done. So what should we do now?"

Based on the noises and serious bouncing that was being generated from inside the moon bounce, anyone standing outside of it and unable to see in might have thought Tim and Rachael were really going at it in there. In actuality, they were only bouncing up and down. Tim watched her blissfully as she bounced because it was truly quite a sight. Everything that should be bouncing was, and the things that really should never bounce didn't because she didn't have any of them. She was trim and tight in all the right places and shapely in all the places that mattered.

Being the conversational master that he was, Tim said, "You look really good when you bounce."

She gave him a sexy smile and they proceeded to gradually bounce over to one another. They reached out and grabbed each other, then slowed their bouncing until they were somehow in synch and gracefully slowed to a stop. They looked deeply into each other's eyes, then kissed. She pulled her lips from his and guided his body down to the floor of the moon bounce with her and they lay side-by-side making out.

Rachael rolled on top of him, kissing him deeper. Things grew even more passionate with the kissing and the groping until Rachael pulled back panting, and whispered that the kids were due there any minute, and it might not be such a great idea for a group of kids to come walking into the backyard to find her screwing some guy.

Tim got the message, blinked his eyes to clear his head a little, and exhaled, "Yeah."

They stood and tried to pull themselves together as Rachael's gaze was instantly drawn to the unbelievably huge bulge in Tim's shorts and her eyes widened. He saw where she was looking, followed her stare and was genuinely impressed right along with her. She looked up to his face and said, "Wow, you're..." Then she looked at it again and added, "Oh, really wow. I hate to leave you like this."

"I'd better go hide," he joked. "Don't want to scar the kids for life."

Rachael seemed captivated, but finally tore her eyes away from it and back to Tim's face and said, "My mother is driving the kids home after, so I can stay and clean up." Then she moved over close to him, "Do you want to... help me clean up?"

"I really love to clean. A lot."

She almost kissed him, then pushed him away and said, "Go."

twenty one - I think it grew a little too much

The party was, of course, a huge hit due to the pool, the moon bounce and the pizza. When it was over, Rachael walked her children and mother to their car while Tim leaned back on the steps in the foyer, a little exhausted, drinking a beer.

When Rachael returned from outside, she closed the door and looked at him apologetically. "They're finally gone."

Tim gave her a sarcastic look and said, "Oh, so soon. It's only been like, six hours."

She put one foot on the step between his legs and leaned in close to him while reaching out with her hand. He handed over the beer and she looked him straight in the eye as she slowly brought it to her lips, took a seductive swig and said, "Your patience will be rewarded." (There really isn't anything sexier than a girl taking a beer from you and slowly putting it to her lips and taking a sip, is there?) Tim watched her in ecstasy, and he felt the blood rushing to his groin.

She climbed up one more step, leaned in close to his ear, handed him the beer, and said, "Just so you know, I don't normally sleep with guys so soon. But you really outdid yourself with this party and..." She lowered her voice to a whisper. "I've been wet since the moon bounce."

He looked at her, a little shocked by the remark. "I have it till tomorrow afternoon, if you…"

She didn't wait for him to finish but slipped right past him up the stairs. He leaned back to watch her upside down, then spun around and proceeded to gulp the rest of his beer. She stopped at the top of the stairs, turned back to him and lifted her skirt a little so he could see the sexy panties that she was wearing. He choked a little on his beer at the sight of her in that white silky thong, then he stood up and took three steps at a time to reach her.

In Tim's old bedroom, wearing only underwear, the busy couple tumbled on the bed, making out furiously. Rachael rolled on top, straddling him as they kissed passionately, then she pulled back, catching her breath and said softly, "You have a condom, right?"

"Yeah."

Rachael removed her bra and slid under the sheet as Tim sat on the bed and removed his underwear. He opened the night table drawer, looked in and pulled out the 3-pack of Magnum condoms. He thought he had one left from that night with Jessica, but he found the box empty. He started playing the sessions with Jessica over in his mind. Once in the living room and then once the next morning. Or was it twice the next morning? He could not remember. He frantically searched the drawer hoping the last one had fallen out of the box, but all he could find was a full box of Minis and he said, "Shit."

"What is it?"

"I uh, only have this one brand I'm not crazy about. Did you bring any?"

"No."

He said completely unconvincingly, "These'll be fine."

Tim grabbed a condom, turned away from her, opened it, struggled to get it on his huge erection and ripped it. He opened another and more carefully tried to put it on then with a frustrated look pushed down hard. He lost his grip, slapped himself hard right in some sensitive parts, cringed and gritted his teeth in order to avoid screeching like a little girl.

Rachael looked over concerned, but he was still blocking her view and she said, "You okay? Want some help?"

"No, I can get it. Let me try--" Tim said as he grabbed the box, rushed to the bathroom and partially closed the door. Rachael sat up in bed and tried to peer through the opening to see what he was up to.

In the bathroom, Tim looked proudly in the mirror at his giant erection and for a moment forgot his mission. He looked back at the box he was holding and then got back on task. He ripped open one of the tiny Minis and tried from a number of angles unsuccessfully to stretch it over his enormous penis head as he called out to her, "They're just a little tight."

From the bed she yelled to him, "They make large size ones I think."

Tim poked his head through the doorway a little annoyed and said, "I know."

He pulled his head back, closed the door and after a pause began grunting and struggling. Rachael looked a little frightened as she reacted to the sounds.

As his fight continued, Tim said, "Just... Get... on there." He was finally able to stretch one of the Mini's and get it successfully over the head of his penis, but he felt unable to breathe and was in excruciating pain. He paused, then slowly tried to roll it down his penis with a look on his face like his dick was caught in a vise. Then it broke, too, with a loud snap. Tim let out a stream of expletives. He grabbed a towel and held it over his groin and returned to the bedroom, where Rachael sat staring at the wall. She eyed him strangely and said hesitantly, "You sure you don't want me to try?"

He walked over to her sheepishly, gave her the box and she looked them over and said, "No wonder. These say snug fit." She opened the package, extracted the condom and held it with both hands like she had done this a few times before. She looked at him, waiting for him to present it for the official covering. He looked at her, bit his lip, closed his eyes and then removed the towel. She looked down at his giant penis and her eyes shot fully open. She dropped the condom, and without taking her eyes off the monster she said, "Oh my God. Wow. Why are you buying small condoms when it's..." She continued to stare at it while feeling on the sheets blindly for the fallen condom.

He admitted, "Those actually used to fit," as he got into bed next to her, pulled the sheets up to his chest and looked to the ceiling exhaling deeply. His erection was tenting the sheets quite unbelievably.

Rachael said, "Those fit? Maybe when you were like eleven."

"No, last week..."

She looked at him confused as he glanced at her, paused and continued reluctantly, "I took these pills and it... Well it started to grow."

Rachael peeked under the sheets for another look and came up frightened then slid away from him slightly and said, "I think it grew a little too much."

Tim pulled his gaze from the ceiling and glared at her as she continued, "Do they even make condoms that size? It's kind of scary big. I'm not sure I'd want to--"

He closed his eyes for a moment, sighed and said, "Okay, first my girlfriend breaks up with me because it's too small, and now you're telling me it's too big. I wish you women knew what you wanted." He folded his arms like a spoiled child and as she looked at him a little bewildered he added, "And I went to all this trouble on the party and now--"

And this was the absolute worst possible thing he could have said and before it was halfway out of his mouth he knew it, but he couldn't stop himself. She glared at him and shot back, "And now what? You did all this just to sleep with me?"

"No, I--", he said as his anger melted away into dread.

She looked at him, shook her head in disbelief as she got out of bed and then really let him have it. "It's a little creepy, you doing all this for a child's birthday party. What are you some kind of pervert?" She stared at him, waiting for a response as she grabbed her bra off the bed and began hooking it back on.

Tim went back to being pissed off at her and said, "Creepy? You used me for your little party. I'll bet you even put your daughter up to asking me."

She glared at him as he looked at her with a cocky stare. "For the first time in my life I have women asking me out, but I was saving myself for you. If you can't handle the new Tim, there are plenty of other women who can."

"You wanna know what your problem is?"

"What?"

"Your dick is now bigger than your brain."

Rachael walked over to where her skirt lay on the floor and picked it up. As she attempted to put it on, she lost her balance and bounced off the closet doors striking the handle down in the process. The door popped open and the pink inflatable cushion shot out onto the floor, along with an avalanche of the other sex paraphernalia. She slipped and landed on the cushion face to face with the attached dildo. She looked at it horrified, then scanned the other items in shock. She stood up and looked at him revolted. "What's wrong with you?"

Equally shocked and embarrassed by the display he said, "Those are my mom's. I swear."

She stood, made some kind of exhaling grunting type of noise indicating that she found him incorrigible, glared at him, then stormed out of the room.

He sat in bed frowning as he heard the door slam, a car start and speed away. He looked over to the night table, spotted the keys to the BMW and grinned.

twenty two - It's good to be Tim

As the garage door opened, the BMW's engine roared, the radio blasted Survivor's 'Eye of the Tiger,' and the convertible top began retracting as the brake lights brightened the otherwise dark driveway. The reverse lights fired up, the car backed out a few feet and then stalled, killing the music and lights. Tim tried twice unsuccessfully to restart the car, but on the third try it finally turned over and the music and lights kicked back on and he was off.

As he drove, Tim thought that if Rachael didn't want him, he would find another hot chick who did. She should have taken one look at his manhood and forgotten all about condoms, and dove right on it with her mouth and everything else she had. If she wasn't interested, it was her loss. Who was she to tell him he was too big? In fact, he didn't think he was quite done with those pills. He'd been gaining about an inch a day since he started taking MaxiManhood and considering the way things had progressed so far, he figured he would reach his target size in just a few more days.

At the pub, Tim sat at the bar between two attractive young women. He was mid-conversation with the one on his right and she appeared, at least partially, interested in what he had to say. With a few drinks in him and a cocky look on his face, he whispered something in her ear. She looked at him appalled, scoffed, then walked away. Unfazed, he turned to the young woman sitting on his left. He got her attention and chatted her up. This one smiled at him initially, but when Tim put his hand over hers her smile faded. He leaned in to her and said something which caused her to look to his crotch. She pulled away then poured her drink slowly into his lap. He calmly dabbed his shorts with a napkin, then turned to scope out the rest of the bar. He spotted a hot, slutty-dressed girl across the room and headed over. When he reached her, she smiled and surprised him when she spoke first. "I've been waiting for you. You looked so good over there I was about to come to you."

Under the moonlit night at the Garrett house backyard, Tim and the slutty girl stood on opposite sides of the pool staring at each other like two drunken, horny morons. She looked into his eyes as she removed her shirt then her bra, revealing gorgeous tits and he stared at them as he quickly removed his shirt and shorts. Starting at her neck, she traced a line with both index fingers between her breasts to her belly button just above the waistband of her skirt. She paused, looked at him and then pushed both thumbs into her skirt and slowly slid them away from each other until they were resting at her hips. He watched her, mesmerized. She slowly peeled the skirt down her hips and bent forward to slide it down her long, firm legs. Wearing only panties, she jumped into the pool and swam over to his side, looked up at him and swirled her tongue over her parted lips. He dove in over her and flipped back under water and came up to face her. He swam back to her and they met in the shallow end of the pool.

They kissed. She ran her hands down his chest into the water and then to his underwear. When she felt what was going on down there, she quickly pulled her lips from his and attempted to peer below the surface. After she spotted his impressive bulge, she looked at him, astonished. She slipped her hands into his underwear and they both gasped. She pulled his expanding penis out of his boxers, wrapped both hands around it and strained to get a better look at it under the water. She brought her gaze back up to his face and smiled, he raised his eyebrows a little smugly, then they kissed more passionately.

The next morning, Tim woke to find that the hot slutty girl had slipped away already, but she did leave a note next to him saying she had a great time and asking him to call her. Tim got out of bed all smiles, walked into the bathroom and gazed in the mirror. He moved in close to check his hair growth and then backed up and flexed his muscles. The cocktail of pills was still working its magic as his hair continued to fill in on top, his belly fat continued to melt away and his muscle tone was still increasing.

He slipped on a pair of shorts and worked out in the basement. He alternated sets of push-ups and sit-ups then performed dumbbell curls and pull-ups. He headed for the kitchen, winded and pumped, and grabbed a bottle of water.

He sat in the great room at his 'measuring station' with his ruler, lotion and a *Glamour* magazine. He flipped through the magazine until he reached an advertisement of a hot super model wearing such a thin shirt that the gorgeous outline of her breasts and hard nipples were clearly visible. He placed the magazine on the sofa next to him and went to work on himself. When he reached his full potential, he placed the ruler next to his prize and smiled. He was just half an inch shy of his twelve-inch goal. He looked at it proudly, then leaned forward and opened each of the three pill bottles and swallowed them down with the bottled water.

Tim went out again that night and picked up another random girl for yet another romp with him and his new super dick. When he walked this one to the door, Tim wore a Hugh Hefner style robe as he kissed her goodbye on the front porch. The surveillance team was still watching the white house, but had taken a keen interest on Tim's activities as well. The officers watched him on the porch as he said his goodbyes to the girl, and both wore a jealous frown. They shared a look that said, 'who does this asshole think he is?' after they witnessed the arrogant look on Tim's face as he watched his latest conquest stroll away.

Back at work, in the conference room, Tim confidently explained and drew out a concept on the white board while George, Bev and a few others looked on. Bev for some reason now seemed captivated either by the idea, Tim's ass, or both. Bev asked him a question about his plan and when he went over the details, she grinned at him dreamily. George noticed Bev's sudden interest in Tim and looked at her with a slightly troubled expression.

Tim noticed it as well, but tried to look casual, even though Bev's shift toward him was really freaking him out.

Tim walked through the halls at the end of the day and was getting stares and greetings from women who never before seemed to know that he existed. He replied to the greetings, walked with a newfound confidence and left the building smiling. This had been his best day at work ever.

Back at home, Tim returned from a run and headed to the back of the house. He stripped off his shirt, shoes and socks and jumped in the pool. He climbed on a float, leaned back with his hands behind his head and realized that for the first time ever, he really was enjoying his life.

twenty three - Which of these is bigger?

At the drug superstore, Tim walked boldly down the Women's Health/condom aisle and past two women shopping there. He moved to the condom section and studied the shelf, but this time he didn't care who was watching him.

He grabbed a box of Magnum XLs in one hand and a box of Durex Supers in the other and looked them over. He paused, then carried both boxes toward the pharmacy counter.

When he reached the counter, he found several customers standing around waiting for their prescriptions. The pharmacist was a cranky middle-aged, ex-military-type looking guy. When Tim tried to make eye contact with him, the ex-soldier did his best to avoid him, but after putting him off repeatedly he reluctantly muttered, "Can I help you?"

Tim cheerily held up both boxes of condoms. "Do you know which of these is bigger?" A few customers took an interest in Tim, his purchase and bold question, and looked on intrigued.

The pharmacist looked at the boxes that Tim was holding and said a little sarcastically, "Bigger?"

Tim held up the Magnums and said, "I've tried these, but I'm really not happy with them." Then he held up the Durexes. "I was hoping maybe these were larger."

The pharmacist scowled at him, opened his hands to take the boxes and Tim handed them over. The pharmacist looked them over and said in a tired voice, "So, are we talking length or girth?"

Tim took a moment and then said, "Both I guess."

The pharmacist paused and just looked through him. "But if you HAD to pick one?"

Tim looked down at himself as if he could actually see what was going on in his pants and the pharmacist shot a look to the gawking customers that said, 'Can you fucking believe this guy?'

Tim looked around and saw that his exchange was garnering quite a lot of notice from the nearby customers. Completely un-rattled by the attention he said, "Um, girth. Wait. No, length."

The pharmacist stopped, smiled and considered that this might be some kind of practical joke on him. He looked around for a group of boys laughing it up at his expense and found no one. He lost the smile and said, "Then I would go with the Magnums," as he handed Tim back the boxes.

Tim thanked the man and casually walked away.

As Tim approached the checkout area he found the self-checkout working and available, but he also spotted Emily working at another register with a woman already in her line. He got into Emily's line and placed the condoms on the belt with a confident smile. Emily recognized him and smiled as the woman in front of him left with her bags. As the belt started rolling the condoms toward Emily, she said, "Hey, it's you."

"Hey."

She looked down at the condoms, picked them up, grinned at him and said, "New boyfriend?"

He glared at her, then looked around a little flustered and said quietly, but sternly, "What? No. They're for me."

"Aren't you a little old to be just now gliding through puberty?" She paused for a second, thinking, then gave him a sour look and added a little too loudly, "Wait, you had that penis surgery." Nearby employees and customers began to stare at them. Tim looked uncomfortable as Emily looked around, noticed the attention and whispered to him, "You know, where they inject the fat--"

Tim waved his hand at her in a gesture to knock it off and he said, "No. No." He looked around at the gaping people and gave them an icy stare until they returned to their own business. Then he leaned in close to Emily and confessed, "If you must know, I've been taking this pill. This enhancement pill."

She gave him a strange look, "Not because of what happened your last trip in here?"

"No, my girlfriend broke up with me because of that and maybe a few other things, but--"

"She sounds like a bitch."

"Oh, she is," he said casually.

Emily gave him a skeptical look. "So, this pill actually worked?"

"Uh, like you wouldn't believe." He gave her a look bordering on creepy and she rolled her eyes a little.

"Don't you feel weird about it? Like it's not really you?"

"What do you mean? It is really me. I'm really happy."

She didn't look convinced. "You need to be happy with who you are. Or were. Whatever freak show science project you have brewing in your pants is not going to make you happy. And whoever you find that likes you for who you're pretending to be is not going to be worth it."

He narrowed his eyes at her, looked away for a moment then back to her and said, "Who are you?"

She smiled at him a little too bubbly and said, "A part-time cashier and full-time psych major."

Tim gave her a look as she waited for him to return the smile. When he didn't, she pursed her lips, scanned the box and put the condoms in a bag and said, "It's 9.59."

Quietly he said, "You just couldn't let me have my moment could you? I came in here in a great mood and now…" His words trailed off as he gave her a frown and handed over a ten.

Emily shrugged and with a guilty look on her face she took the money and returned the change.

"I'm gonna go back to shopping online," Tim said as she handed him the bag.

As he turned to walk away she called after him, "Don't do that."

He turned back. "Every time I'm in here we have this same conversation about my… Are you this way with everyone who buys these?"

"Oh yes, I take a vested interest in all my condom customers," she said, while giving him a serious look. He fought to hold back the slight grin that was forming on his face and managed to scowl back at her, but when her look turned to a sweet smile, he bit his lips together in a desperate attempt to not give anything away.

"Thanks," he said.

"I hope I see you again soon. If you run out of those or something. Well, I hope you don't run out of those too soon. I mean, you should be careful. Actually, I don't know what I'm saying and I'm going to stop now."

She looked away embarrassed and for the first time she was the one who ended up feeling uncomfortable in one of their little conversations. Tim enjoyed the change. When she looked back at him, he grinned slightly and she looked away shyly, still a little flustered. He studied her face and she looked different to him now. He couldn't explain what had changed, but she was really starting to grow on him. Before he turned to go, he said, "Okay, so..." and when she finally looked back at him, he continued, "I'll see you."

twenty four - What the fuck are you taking them for? You can barely get through the door as it is.

On the basketball court, Tim, Carter and four other guys warmed up by taking shots. Rick rushed in, looked around nervously and approached Tim, who was kneeling down tying his shoes.

"I need to talk to you," Rick demanded.

Tim got up and patted Rick on the shoulder and said, "Later."

Tim played better than he had ever played before. He was on fire, hitting nearly three quarters of his shots, making moves he didn't know he had as the other guys looked on, astounded. He was putting on a clinic while Rick, who was usually one of the strongest players on the court, was remarkably bad.

Tim especially enjoyed the games that day since he was showing up Rick at every opportunity. In the first game, Tim jogged to the three-point line, got a pass, and nailed a quick turnaround jumper right in Rick's face. In the second game, Rick took a ridiculously long shot that was embarrassingly far off the mark. Carter grabbed the rebound and rushed down the court with Tim following close behind. As if they had planned it, Carter tossed the ball up off the backboard where Tim grabbed the alley-oop and layed it off the glass for an easy, yet impressive, score as the rest of the guys watched in awe.

Near the end of the third game, Jill entered the building and watched from the door. Carter passed Tim the ball, he faked a shot, Rick jumped up, badly fooled, and Tim dribbled around him for an easy lay-up that sealed the victory. Jill took the whole scene in. She spotted Rick bent over with his hands on his knees looking exhausted and defeated and when Rick's eyes met hers, she shook her head then looked away, disappointed.

Tim headed back to the middle of the court super-pumped and as he approached Rick he said, "Eat-it biaaaaatch."

Rick looked up to Tim, crushed, and as Tim's team rushed toward the door smiling, Rick's team stayed behind arguing.

Jill watched Tim approach as other guys complimented him on his play. She looked down shyly as if she expected him to stop. He walked right past her as she said, "Nice shot." When she looked up, she was standing there alone, watching Tim walk away.

After his shower, Tim stood at his locker dressing while the other guys were still in the shower room. Rick entered with the rest of his team and while his teammates undressed and headed to the showers, Rick sat on the bench obviously pretending to struggle with the laces on his shoes. Then he moved on to search for some mysterious item in his bag that never emerged. When they were finally alone, Rick rushed over to Tim and said, "I've been taking those pills."

"What pills?" Tim said taken aback.

"That Maxi… MaxiManhood crap."

"What the fuck are you taking them for? You can barely get through the door as it is."

Rick smiled and said, "You can never be big enough, right? Anyway, I've got a question."

His smile melted away and he moved closer to Tim and said quietly, "Did it shrink at first?"

Tim narrowed his eyes, confused. "What?"

"When you started the pills, did it get smaller at first?"

Tim thought it over then Rick smirked at him, "Wait, if yours got smaller, it would have disappeared. Right?"

Tim glared at him and turned away. Rick stood behind him waiting with a sorry desperate expression while a slightly evil grin formed on Tim's face. Then Tim paused, he put on a serious expression and looked back to Rick, "It did. It did get smaller. That's when you need to double the dose."

Rick pondered this with a child-like look on his face and Tim fought to suppress a smirk. He knew Rick took a lot of supplements. It was obvious to Tim that the cocktail of supplements he was ingesting was interacting with the 'effective' ingredient in the penis pill and causing adverse side effects. It was also obvious to Tim that doubling the dose was probably the worst possible advice he could give. A few guys returned from showering as Tim slipped on his shirt. Rick backed away from him, narrowed his eyes and said just to confirm, "Really double it?"

Tim said with as much mock confidence as he could muster, "Yeah, then you really start seeing results." Rick looked at him a little skeptically. Tim made the sound of an explosion and gestured an explosive blast with his hands while nodding his head, then Rick looked at him semi-convinced.

Tim grabbed his bag as Rick pulled down his shorts and stood uncomfortably close to his locker in an attempt to shield all view of his brand new problem. Rick glanced back to see if anyone was looking at him and nearly fell into his open locker in the process. He steadied himself, then quickly wrapped a towel around his waist. He turned to look at Tim and Tim gave him a confident thumbs-up. Tim turned away and headed out the door as the smile widened on his face.

In the parking lot, Tim headed to his car, still wearing a huge smile, as Jill leaned on Rick's car. When she spotted him, she rushed over to walk next to him. "Good game today."

He gave her a brief casual glance. "Yeah, it feels good to finally beat those guys."

She eyed him while drinking in the whole new 'Tim' package. "You look different. Your hair..."

He said confidently, "The Rogaine's finally kicking in," and stopped in front of the BMW. He hit a few buttons on the remote so the car unlocked and the convertible top popped up and started folding away.

She looked on amazed, then stepped closer to the car and looked inside, impressed, and said, "This is nice."

Tim slid into the car, put on his sunglasses and started her up. She looked him over once more. "Something else is different about you. What is it?"

He ignored the question and brushed her off with a quick, "Thanks. See ya," as he pulled away.

Back at work, Tim sat at his desk and over the next hour he noticed Kelly repeatedly walking past his door. He normally wouldn't see her more than once a week on his side of the building, and never five times in one day. When he noticed her pass and attempt to make eye contact with him, he finally called out to her. A moment after he did, she appeared at his door and leaned against the frame, smiled and casually said, "Oh hey, Tim."

"Is that happy hour still on tonight?"

"It is. You going?" she said, suddenly a little perkier. She stepped into his office and started nervously running her fingers over the doorknob.

"I'll see you there."

"Would you give me ride over?" she said, looking right at him as she fooled with the doorknob. He watched her touch it and somehow it was the sexiest thing he had ever seen. After a long pause of him not answering, she called his name and jolted him out of his trance.

He tore his eyes back to her face and said, "No problem. "

twenty five - This is fun... but do you think we can come up with a safe word?

After Tim watched Kelly slide her gorgeous ass into the BMW, he climbed in and started the car. As he put on his sunglasses she said, "I left my license at home. Would you mind stopping by there first?"

Kelly's apartment was small, but her bed was big and it just happened to be the first and only stop when she gave Tim the tour of the place. They weren't in the apartment more than five minutes before the clothes started flying. They were both nearly naked with her straddling him in bed while she kissed his chest. He wore only boxer briefs while she was in a matching bright yellow lace bra and panties. She slowly moved down his body, kissing every inch of it along the way, until she reached his stomach. Once there, she looked him in the eye, licked her lips and whispered, "I want to do everything to you."

He swallowed hard and said, "Do, uh, anything you want."

She ran her tongue just above the waistband of his boxer briefs from one side of his body to the other, then looked up again and said, "You like to be tied up?" She didn't wait for an answer, but instead ran her tongue back to just under his belly button, paused, then inserted it under the waistband of his boxers and flicked it back and forth. This sent shivers all over his body as he lay helplessly on her bed with his hands gripping the sheets in an effort to keep his head from exploding off his body. She lifted her head up, looked him in the eye. "Can I tie you up?"

"Yeah," he said and nodded his approval while breathing heavily.

"Turn over," she commanded and he looked to her a little confused, but still under her spell. She rose up off him to allow him to turn over and he did. She pulled a padded leather handcuff up from the side of the bed, seemingly out of nowhere, and attached it to his hand and then she vaulted like a Romanian Gymnast to the other side of the bed, pulled up another handcuff and secured it.

"Oh, you have them ready," Tim said, quietly and a little disturbed.

She kissed her way along his back, slowly pulled his boxers down, then roughly spread his legs apart one at a time.

"Whoa, what are you--" is all he could manage before she quickly cuffed one leg and then the other. She paused, looking at him panting in that vulnerable position. She knelt between his legs, reached in between his thighs and slid them apart a little more for a better look and commented, "Wow, they weren't kidding."

Tim's nervousness grew as he stammered, "Huh, what who wasn't..." as she leaped off the bed.

Kelly looked back at him and added, "I'm not sure I have the right size."

"Right size?" he asked nervously, then paused. "This is fun... but do you think we can come up with a safe word?"

Kelly entered the closet. Tim tested the straps and boy they were tight. He struggled briefly then relaxed, shook his head and smiled while trying to think only good thoughts.

From the closet, Kelly yelled back, "Did Zach give me a safe word?"

His smiled faded a little with her reply and the tone in her voice. "Who's Zach?" he said casually, trying to mask his concern, as she emerged from the closet wearing a strap-on harness and carrying a case. Tim struggled to turn enough on one side and then the other in order to get a look and repeated with a little more unease, "Who's Zach?"

She placed the case on the bed and opened it. Inside were neatly organized dildoes ordered from smallest to largest. She admired her collection and said in a calm, but frightening voice, "Just an old boyfriend; a well-hung old boyfriend. Kinda like you. He introduced me, really he forced me into the wonderful world of bondage."

Kelly studied the attachments in the case and took another look between Tim's legs. She rolled her eyes and asked him, "Are you hard? Sorry it was so big already that I forgot to check."

"What?"

"Never mind, I'll check it myself," she said as she climbed on the bed, sat right on the back of his head and reached between his legs with both hands roughly massaging his cock then added, "Wow it's already huge, but you're not quite there."

Tim started to almost enjoy what she was doing as her eyes widened and she stared at it open mouthed as it grew even further and said, "Okay, but I don't know..." She climbed off him and returned to the case.

He looked back at her alarmed and said, "Those, uh, things. Are those for you?"

She walked up to him, kneeled next to the bed and leaned close to his face and said, "No, they're for you. I'm going to show you what it's like to be with someone just your size." Her voice took on a sort of serial killer scary edge as she added, "Just like that fucking prick Zach did to me."

She stood and walked back to the case as Tim tested the straps again, yanking them hard, as he whined, "I really don't want to do this."

She said in a mocking sweet voice, "But you said I could do anything."

"I thought you were talking about a blowjob or something!" He struggled to get a better look in the case and when he did he said, "You, uh, got some really big ones."

She tossed the largest one down in front of his face and it landed with a loud thump. He eyed it, horrified, as she said, "None do you justice, but this is the closest. I call him Kong."

Tim pleaded, "Funny story. Two weeks ago I was actually really, uh, small. I took this enlargement pill. Just call my ex-girlfriend Jill Taylor. Seriously."

With that, Kelly looked at him smiling and said, "Wait, you're Jill's Tim? Tim, ten year-old boy, Tim? I'm serious. I have one named after you. I'm not even kidding." Then she reached into her case and pulled out the smallest one and pointed it at him. "Big Tim meet Little Timmy."

She paused to ponder this for a second, and then said, "Okay, maybe that changes things a little. Why don't we vote on which to use? Kong or here's Little Timmy." She laid the small one near his head and Tim looked at it, a little insulted.

"I was a little bigger than that," he said cockily.

She looked back to the case and said, "Oh, then I have bigger ones we can—"

"No, no. That one is actually pretty close. It's good," he said, losing the attitude.

"Okay, you vote first," she said.

"Do we really have to do this?"

In a voice one would use when scolding a child, she said, "So if you don't want a vote, then I'll just go ahead and choose for--"

"No. Okay, I... uh choose Tiny Tim."

"Little Timmy," she corrected him.

"Yes. Yes, Little Timmy," he pleaded.

She pretended to actually give it some thought and said, "Well, I… I think I choose... Kong."

Tim swallowed hard as she picked up a bottle of lube and a latex glove from her case and said, "Let's see. So that's one vote for Little Timmy, and one vote for Kong."

He watched as she took her time slipping on the glove. She adjusted each finger individually and then gave him a nod. She squeezed a large dollop of lube onto two fingers from the nearly empty bottle and he turned his face away, bracing for the worst, and said, "Uh, what are you doing?"

"Getting you ready, silly."

She roughly jammed two lubed fingers into the place he and maybe ninety-eight percent of the male population most dreaded having fingers jammed into. And she really worked it in there good as he buried his head into the mattress and let out a muffled scream. She said, "I'm going to need more of this, especially if the next round of voting goes the way I think it will." She climbed off the bed and Tim gave a quick violent struggle to free his hands, but it was no use. He exhaled and said, "How about this. Use Tiny, I mean Little Timmy, this time then I promise I'll come back another day and we'll go with Kong. I promise."

"That's not gonna work for me. Give it some more thought and we'll re-vote, but if it's tied again then I'll get two votes in the next round," she said then she carried the empty lube bottle away and entered the closet.

Tim turned his head to the other side and found he was inches away and looking right at the giant head of the mammoth Kong. He shuddered and called out to her, "What about that safe word?" Then he struggled hard against the straps, whimpering like a puppy.

twenty six - What the hell happened to you?

Tim entered the pub and there was really no other way to characterize it; he looked like shit. His hair was a complete mess, his clothes were wrinkled, his shirt was buttoned incorrectly and he walked just a little funny. Carter was sitting on a bar stool and he watched as Tim slowly made his way to the bar. When Tim was beside him Carter's eyes-widened and he said, "What the hell happened to you?"

Tim ignored the question, slid onto a barstool next to Carter and slumped with his elbows resting on top of the bar. He shuffled around on the stool in an attempt to get comfortable, grimaced in pain, then stood instead. Carter looked him over concerned, "Were you in an accident or something?"

Tim gave him a tired look. "I wish."

"So, what happened to you two? Everybody's gone." Carter took a pull from his beer and smirked at him. "You boned her, didn't you? And judging from your condition, she was too much for you; way, way too much. So, how was it?"

Tim just looked at him, paused to think, then said casually, "I'd have to say the highlight was the prostate exam." Tim motioned for the bartender to bring him a beer.

Carter gave him a knowing smile, "Yeah, she gave you the little old pinky in the backdoor. There's nothing like a little ass play to mix things up and--"

Tim said a little too loudly, "Would you shut up for a fucking second? She tied me up like a freaking animal. She strapped me down and was preparing to fuck me, Carter. I mean like she..." Tim looked around the bar to be sure no one was listening and then he quietly continued, "She was going to strap one on and then..." Tim looked at him with a contorted face and raised eyebrows, which is somehow the universal facial sign for anal rape.

Carter's smile faded and he said, "Shit, then what happened?" as the bartender arrived with a beer for each of them.

Tim took a long drink then looked Carter in the eye. "You really want to know what happened?" Carter nodded as if he never wanted to hear a story more.

Tim told the story in incredible detail. Carter was captivated and asked a lot of questions, mostly about Kelly and what she was wearing. When Tim reached the part just before the so-called prostate exam, he took a sip of beer then paused to collect his thoughts while he stared down at the bar.

"Yeah, so, then what happened?" Carter said with growing impatience.

Tim snapped out of it, looked Carter in the eye and plowed ahead. "Okay, so I was tied up tight, she put on this rubber glove and she squirted some of the lube on her fingers and she, she violated me. It felt like she stuck her whole freaking hand up there or something. But thank God the bottle she was using was empty. So she went into the closet for another bottle. She must not have been able to find it easily because she was gone a long time and I started pulling at the straps and trashing around on the bed. I pulled hard and one of the hand straps came loose. I couldn't believe it because those straps were really tight. So I stopped struggling, checked to be sure she was still occupied in the closet and she was. I quietly unbuckled the other hand strap and managed to get one leg strap undone. Then I turned and looked into the closet and she was looking right at me. She was kneeling in there and made eye contact with me. It was freaky. I'll never forget the way she looked at me."

Tim took another sip of beer and glanced at Carter, who was on the edge of his seat, still fascinated by the story. After a few seconds Carter gave him an annoyed look and said, "So what the hell happened?"

"Well, I didn't have time to unbuckle the last strap, so I dove off the bed toward the closet with one leg still strapped to the bed. When I did, I must have knocked the dildo case to the floor because dildoes were everywhere. There was enough slack in the leg strap that I was able to reach the closet door and I slammed it shut with her still in there."

Carter looked him over impressed. "Dude you're like fucking Jason Bourne."

"I know," Tim said nodding while they shared a look. "So from inside the closet I heard her say, 'Uh, Tim what are you doing?' And she tried to open the door, but I kept pushing back on it to keep it closed with one hand while I used the other hand to unbuckle my leg."

Tim ordered another beer and continued, "Her door had one of those handles, you know not the knobs, but the…"

Carter gave him a hand gesture that said he got it and to hurry him along.

"And so I was able to hold it steady with one hand so she couldn't get out. If she had like, a regular knob, I don't think I would have been able to keep her in there."

Carter nodded, mesmerized as Tim took another sip of beer. "So I freed my leg and then slid my back against the door just as she tried slamming her body hard on the other side. Man she is one strong chick. The door popped open an inch or so a few times with her pounding on it and a couple times it nailed me right in the head, but she wasn't able to open it."

"How did you get out of there?" Carter asked.

"I didn't know what to do. I was completely naked and my clothes were across the room. I couldn't just run out of there like that and I wasn't sure what else she had in that closet. Maybe she had a baseball bat or something. If I had just gone for my clothes, she probably would have... I don't know. So I looked around the room searching for something to use to block her in the closet, maybe a chair or something, but there wasn't anything. But then I saw one of the dildoes and got an idea. It was out of my reach, so I tried to move it closer with my foot. The whole time she was saying shit like, 'I'm serious. Let me out of here. I'm not even kidding.' You know how she talks."

They both shared a nod and Tim plowed ahead, "She kept pounding on the door. So I was able to slide the dildo closer to me with my foot, I grabbed it and wedged it under the door, balls side down and it created like this... uh... "

Carter smiled and said, "Fucking MacGyver'esque makeshift door stop."

Tim returned the smile. "Yeah."

Carter looked at him, stunned. They both downed the rest of their beers and then Tim went on, "So Kelly pushed the door one more time really, really, hard and I lost my grip on the handle and the door opened a few inches and then it was stuck. The dildo had wedged under the door on both sides and now it wouldn't move either way. So I stood up and looked at her as she peered out the small gap in the door. She backed away and then pushed hard on it again, but it wouldn't budge. I grabbed my clothes and began putting them on. Then she said something like, 'Tim, I really wasn't going to do anything,' and I just cut her off and said, 'You need some fucking professional help.' Then, get this, I actually said, 'Like some really good help. I'm serious. I'm not even kidding.' And I got the hell out of there."

As Tim wrapped up the story, Carter simply stared straight ahead at the bottles of liquor on the wall. Then he slowly turned his head and looked at Tim with a funny expression and said, "But how will she get out?"

"The front door is unlocked. I'm sure someone will hear her."

"She's at Glen Oaks. First floor right?"

Tim took another sip of beer then eyed Carter suspiciously. "Yeah, that's right."

Carter tried to look casual as he said, "If she's on the first floor, then someone will definitely hear her. Yeah." Then he stood up looked at the watch-less wrist and added unconvincingly, "Oh, man I'm late. I just remembered this thing I, uh..."

With that, Carter turned away and Tim watched him as he walked toward the door. Tim loudly said, "It's 1C."

Carter looked back to him, busted. "Thanks."

The bartender dropped off another beer. Tim took a sip then shook his head smiling as he watched Carter walk out the door.

twenty seven - Jesus Ladies, I'm up here!

The next day at work, Tim waited outside the conference room while a meeting was wrapping up inside. Down the hall a woman and Bev were talking. Bev spotted Tim and approached him wearing a strange smile. "I wanted to get more information on your presentation from the other day."

"Sure, I can put something in writing and have it to you by the end of the day."

"No, that won't be necessary. Just come by my office at three." Then she walked away as Tim watched her, confused.

At two fifty-nine Bev was on the phone at her desk in her large executive office. Tim appeared at the door, legal pad in hand. She saw him and motioned for him to enter. As he approached the desk she waved him over to the sofa. He hesitated, then walked to the sofa and took a seat. Bev cut her call off early, hung up, smiled at him, then walked over to close the door. Tim watched as she locked the door and he swallowed hard. She turned toward him, paused, and eyed him hungrily. After checking the lock on the door, she sauntered over and sat next to him as he squirmed uneasily on the sofa.

Tim eyed her strangely and said, "I came up with, uh, a, uh, few... new ideas."

She put her meaty paw around the back of the couch and slid closer to him, squishing him into the sofa's arm. He placed the legal pad in his lap with his elbows uncomfortably stuck to his sides and said, "First, I, uh, think if we modify the software to--"

Bev gently ran her finger on the notebook over his groin and softly said, "I like this idea. Right here."

Tim jumped up and took a few steps to the center of the room. She followed him and he moved further away until he was trapped between her desk and a row of chairs that extended to a wall of windows.

"You see, I have a big problem," Bev said as she sat in the chair in front of him, blocking him in. With the wall on one side and her legs on the other, he was left with no other options short of jumping over her, so he leaned back and took an awkward seat on the edge of her desk.

She continued, "I can't be satisfied by an average man."

"Well, that's a sh-shame," he stammered.

"The world is filled with average men," Bev added.

"If you look at a bell curve, that's kind of the idea. In college, I minored in probability, so I--"

"I hear that you're anything but."

"No, I'm... You know Rick, he's what you're looking for. I can intro--" he said then stopped when he noticed a printout of an email on her desk. The message had Rachael's name as the sender and Tim proceeded to read it as Bev reached out and ran her hand down his forearm. The email contained a short, not too harsh, paragraph about how inappropriately rude Rachael thought the person was being to her. The first part was a little unprofessional maybe; it might garner someone a stern lecture or possibly a note in his or her personnel file, but that would be about it.

Bev said, "I'm not attracted to Rick." But Tim was too focused on the email to hear her.

The last sentence of the email struck Tim as strange. The message contained an especially harsh sentence that did not seem to fit with the style of the earlier writing, but at the same time it seemed oddly familiar to him. Still he couldn't quiet put his finger on it. It said, 'I should biaaaaatch slap you, you rude fuck.'

"Rick doesn't do it for me," she said, her voice hardening as she began to lose patience with him.

Tim said, preoccupied, "Rick, yeah…" as he re-read the last sentence again. Then he repeated, "Rick," sternly as a knowing smile crossed his face. He picked up the printed email, looked at Bev. "Is this why Rachael was fired?" Before she could answer, he executed a difficult maneuver, which featured a mini leap over her legs followed by a perfect stick of a landing down into the chair beside her.

She looked at him even more impressed, "You are really spry. Are you like this in bed?"

He didn't answer, but instead held the page out for her review. She glanced at it quickly and said curtly, "It is." Then she down shifted to sweetness and added, "That's not important. How does Tim Garrett Assistant Director sound?"

He looked at her, sidetracked, and paused as he tried to wrap his head around the offer. "I have been hoping for a promotion." He looked out the window past her briefly pondering, then shook it off and glanced back down at the page in his hand. "But did you notice anything strange about this email?"

"Yes, it's completely unprofessional."

"I don't think Rachael wrote this," he pleaded.

"Well, she admitted it."

"I mean I don't think she wrote all of this. I don't think she sent it."

He studied the email again and his eyes widened with a brilliant realization and he looked at her. She eyed him up and down and placed a hand on his groin as she said, "What's the probability that you can give me an orgasm with your giant--"

"Can I borrow this? I'll be right back and we can finish. I promise," he said as he stood and backed away from her.

She waved him off, disappointed, and he rushed out of the room.

Outside Rachael's recently vacated cubicle, Tim looked up to the ceiling and found what he was looking for: a security camera pointed toward the entrance to her workstation. He smiled.

Moments later in the security office, Tim held the email as the security officer typed away on the keyboard and using the automated security archive system selected the proper camera and the day in question.

"Go to 11:50 AM," said Tim.

The officer typed as Tim watched the screen intently. His jaw dropped and he smiled when he found exactly what he was hoping for. Tim said loudly, "There! Would you burn that and the next 10 minutes on a DVD for me?"

Tim rushed into Bev's office holding the email and DVD and announced, "Biaaaaatch," and Bev glared at him in shock. Tim gave her an apologetic look, "Oh sorry," then he paused to catch his breath. "Does Rachael strike you as the type of person who would use the term biaaaaatch slap, much less the type of person who would use the lesser know 'five A' spelling?"

"What?" Bev said completely lost.

"I can prove she didn't send this."

Tim slid in behind Bev and leaned into her in order to reach her PC. She slid back slightly which created a little more contact with him as he pushed the button to open the drawer for the DVD player. When he felt her rub against him even more, he gave her an uncomfortable smile and inserted the disc.

The DVD started to play on the computer as she began stroking his forearm. "Do you work out?"

Tim frowned at her, "Could you please just watch this? It's coming up. Here it is." And on her PC screen Rick was clearly seen entering Rachael's cubicle. Tim paused the playback and the time on the footage showed 11:55:32.

Tim held out the hardcopy of the email and pointed out the time it was sent. "Look. The time on the email shows 11:56:18."

Tim fast-forwarded the footage until Rick exited the cubicle laughing hysterically at 11:56:34, then paused it again to point out the time stamp. "You see?"

Tim fast-forwarded until Rachael returned to the cubicle and paused the footage one last time and the time stamp showed 11:58:25. He backed away from her desk smugly, like a lawyer who had just cracked a murder trial wide open with the accused admitting his guilt right on the stand and under oath.

Bev stared at him open-mouthed and said, "You're like Magnum P.I. I have another case for you to solve." She grabbed the email, tossed it behind her and pushed him down on the desk.

Tim held her away by the shoulders and said angrily, "That asshole screwed over a single mother just because she didn't want to date him and this means nothing to you?"

Evidently not, because she began unbuttoning his shirt and said, "I love it when you take charge."

"I'm serious," he said as he glared at her.

She looked him in the eye and gave up on the shirt. She stepped back and took a deep breath. "Okay, so she didn't send it. What do you want me to do?"

Tim gave her look that said *I can't believe I need to explain this.*" Give her back her job."

Bev paused, then gave him a wicked grin. "If I do that, what'll you do for me?"

"Uh, what do you want?" he said hesitantly.

Bev unbuttoned her dress exposing her bulbous freckled cleavage as Tim fought to conceal his growing nausea.

Twenty minutes later, Tim escaped from Bev's office mostly in one piece, at least physically. What happened in there he would never speak of and he would struggle to erase from his mind for a long, long, long time. Even though his eyes were closed through at least eighty-five percent of the encounter, he still had managed to see things that no man should ever be forced to see.

He made his way down the hall looking just a little traumatized as he approached two women talking. They recognized him, smiled, and then focused on his groin. This sent him over the edge. He narrowed his eyes and screamed a little like a mental patient as he pointed to his face, "Jesus ladies, I'm up here!" He ran past them and out the double doors as they shared a frightened look.

twenty eight - There's a first time for everything

After Tim pulled the BMW into the garage, he turned off the ignition, hit the button on the garage door opener and slumped on the steering wheel. The sunlight slowly evaporated into pure darkness as the garage door slowly closed. He remained there in the dark, reflecting on the past twenty-four hours, unsure whether he was more damaged mentally by Kelly's kidnapping and near rape, or his quid pro quo tryst with the robust and deceptively agile Bev. Who the fuck was he kidding? It was Bev, definitely Bev.

Tim suddenly felt like he was about to vomit. He rolled the window down and hung his head out. After a few moments the feeling passed. He pulled his head back in and flipped on the car's interior lights just as a memory came flooding back to him. It was the memory of the night of his prom and his less-than-satisfying first time.

Tim rarely dated in high school, and what little experience he did have with girls was limited to kissing. He had never even felt a girl up before that disastrous night.

Tim had always been shy and awkward around girls, and he believed that this was all due to the fact that he was a late bloomer. Tim didn't even begin to hit puberty until the age of sixteen, a full four years later than most normal boys. And it seemed to be the longest, most drawn out puberty in history. He was all of five foot two and one hundred twenty pounds when he graduated from high school, and looked more like a fourteen year-old boy than someone about to be a college freshman.

He worked with Ashley at a department store. He was mildly attracted to her and she pretty much felt the same. They had spoken a few times at the store, and gone out as a group with the work crowd once or twice. It was two weeks before Ashley's prom and she had just broken up with her current boyfriend. She went to a different high school than Tim, and Tim had no plans to attend his own prom given his limited social standing there. Ashley was the one who did the asking. Tim semi-reluctantly accepted and was soon fitted for a tuxedo, embarrassingly in the boys' section of the rental shop.

Prom was an awkward first date for the couple, but mostly it was uneventful. At an after party, Ashley proceeded to get drunk and make it clear to everyone that she was not over her recent break-up. On the drive home, she seemed mostly out of it until Tim made the turn into her neighborhood. That's when she got her second wind and began massaging his crotch. Shocked, he nearly ran the car over the curb and quickly pulled over as she moved on to unbuckle his belt.

Once the car was stopped, she quickly removed her panties then reached over and pulled him on top of her seemingly effortlessly, as if he were a rag doll. Surprised by her man handling, Tim was initially paralyzed as she began kissing him. Eventually he returned her passion and they began to make out and grope each other. Then she pushed him back a little and said, "Do you have a condom?"

He nodded and fished a condom from his wallet. He then yanked down his boy's size fourteen pants, swiftly opened up the package and slipped it on his small, but super ready penis. With his protection secured, Tim climbed on top of Ashley. As he began his careful thrusting, Tim noticed her face begin to turn a strange, pale greenish color. He ignored it when she rolled down the window. After mere seconds of going at it, Ashley put one hand over her mouth used the other to push Tim away. Then she leaned her head out the window and proceeded to projectile vomit. She made a horrible gut wrenching sound. The volume of her expulsion was quite remarkable, and amazingly most of it escaped the side of the car. Tim grasped his mouth with one hand in an attempt to suppress his own gag reflex and pushed the button to roll the window down with the other to get some much-needed fresh air.

Needless to say, that was the end of the magic night and also of their relationship. Although it lasted just a few clumsy seconds, and the only ejaculating that occurred was on her part and unfortunately out of her mouth, he had done it; his virginity was gone.

twenty nine - Really it shrunk? How much?

Tim shook his head and snapped out of it. It wasn't Ashley who had just been screwing him; it was Bev. He dashed into the house, rushed to the bathroom, stripped off his clothes and climbed in the shower. His attempt to wash away any memory of the recent events failed and he ended up cowered, shivering and curled up in the fetal position on the floor of the shower with the water pounding on his back.

Tim fought the mental visions of what Bev had done to him and worse yet, what she had made him do. He started to question why he did it. Did he really do it for Rachael, the girl who ran away from him and accused him of being a pervert, or did he want to do it? Oh God, he hoped not. He probably could have convinced Bev to give Rachael her job back without, without... he couldn't even bring himself to think it. And how would Bev treat him now? Would she think she could have him whenever she wanted? He would definitely need to find a new job. He cleared his mind, stood to let the water wash over him and decided he would do the only thing that he could do to move on from this. And that was drink a great deal of alcohol. Something like two drinks away from alcohol poisoning would kill just enough brain cells to pull him past this.

While Tim's skin pruned, nearby at the abandoned house, Larry watched the white house where absolutely nothing was happening. He became distracted when he spotted a car drive past the house toward the Garrett place and he followed it up Tim's driveway. Inside the car, he noticed an attractive female. It was Jill, and she was talking to herself. Actually, she appeared to be in the middle of a practice heated argument. She didn't look happy, but damn she looked good. Larry didn't notice her mood, but instead focused with the binoculars on her chest. When she emerged from the car, he said to Sam, "Can you freaking believe he's got another girl?"

After the shower, Tim headed downstairs to the kitchen, wearing only a towel, and grabbed a beer. He had pulled himself together a little, but he was still on edge. This was evidenced by the near heart stopping reaction he had when startled by the doorbell and then loud banging at the front door. He rushed to the foyer and the banging intensified as he approached. He ripped the door open and when he spotted Jill he said, "Jill, what the…"

Jill quickly stepped inside, took the beer right out of his hand and angrily pushed him aside as she walked past him. He said sarcastically, "Would you like something to drink?"

She turned back to him, bit her lip not knowing where to begin, and proceeded to guzzle the beer down. He eyed her strangely and was unsure what to make of her sudden appearance. When she finished the beer, she handed him back the empty bottle, he glanced down at it, rolled his eyes while she glared at him and said, "What'd you do to Rick?"

"What are you talking about?"

"It's his... It shrunk."

"What shrunk?" he said, totally oblivious.

She gave him an irritated stare, but he still appeared lost so she stared at his groin for a second and motioned with her hand until he finally got the message. He sounded a little moronic when he simply said, "Oh." But when the impact of it all finally hit him, Tim began chuckling. Jill looked him over from head to toe in that towel and was unexpectedly distracted by his new body.

In Tim's mind, he flashed back to their breakup, frowned and said with an edge to his voice, "So what's it like now — ten year-old boy sized?"

"What?" she said, a little lost, then she returned to looking him in the eye and snapped back on subject. "He said you put him on this male enhancement pill."

Tim scoffed as she stared at him, waiting for a reply. He narrowed his eyes and said, "I put him on it? What am I his doctor? Look, I'm taking it. It's working for me. He must have looked at the bottle in my gym locker. I can't control what — "

"Did you tell him to double the dose?" she asked as if she already knew the answer. "Did you?"

He paused and then exhaled, "Yeah, but he's a real asshole. I think it must just be karma because..." He didn't finish that thought, but instead glared at her and continued a little angrier this time. "You know, I've seen your new boyfriend at the GNC; he uses a cart for God's sake. He does most of his freaking grocery shopping there! I realize he hasn't eaten any sugar since like, Clinton was in office, but he's also so hopped up on supplements and steroids, that he's lucky to be alive. I've heard that steroids can actually shrink your testicles and if you combine that with all the other crap he was taking, who knows what that hell that could do to you. So don't put this on me."

As he thought about Rick's manhood actually shriveling up and hopefully falling off, the expression on his face from the angry tirade morphed into a grin. "Really though, it shrunk? How much?"

He didn't wait for an answer and said, "Don't tell me. It really doesn't matter." He looked at her and added, "This is the best news I've..." but couldn't finish because he began laughing instead.

She watched him and bit her lip as she fought to hold back her own laughter as she struggled to say, "It's not funny!" But Jill lost it when he held up his thumb and forefinger about two inches apart and gave her a serious quizzical look. She covered her mouth with one hand, shook her head no and used the fingers of her other hand to display back a size estimate that was a little closer to one inch with her eyebrows raised. He gave her a skeptical look, she shook her head yes this time and when she did, they both broke into uncontrollable laughter.

Moments later, as Tim gave Jill a tour of the great room, still wearing only a towel, she noticed the lobster tank and gave it an odd look. "Were those dinner the other night?"

Tim shook his head yes with a slight frown and she gave him an apologetic smile, which melted him a little.

"Where are your parents?" Jill asked.

"On vacation. A cruise."

She looked at his chest. He noticed and crossed his arms self-consciously. She eyed him up and down saying,

"You've been working out." When she stopped on the way back up, staring right at the 'towel' area, she added, "What exactly did this pill do?"

"It's just a little bit... bigger."

"Show me," she demanded as she stepped to him and grabbed the towel with one hand.

He put a hand over hers, stopping her, and said a little playfully, "No way."

"Come on."

"You want me to just pull out my dick? Right here?"

"I've seen it before."

She gave him a look like it was no big deal and he looked to the lobsters for guidance. One lobster lifted its claws seemingly in agreement. Tim paused then pursed his lips, grabbed the towel with one hand and pulled it free. He let it fall to the floor and he didn't bother looking down at it himself. He simply looked right past her, feeling a little self-conscious. When the towel fell, it revealed possibly one of the largest flaccid penises in history. Jill's eyes widened, she moved her head forward a few inches and squinted for a better look. Then she appeared faint.

thirty - Have you noticed your balls?

Moments later, as Jill sat flushed on the sofa, Tim returned carrying a bottle of water with the towel re-secured. He sat next to her, handed her the bottle, and looked at her concerned. "Are you sure you're okay?"

She took a drink, stared at him, smiling gently, and said, "How big does it get?"

"What do you mean?"

She motioned again with her hands, "When it's--"

"I haven't measured it," he said and tried to sound convincing, but failed miserably.

"Yeah. Okay," she said as she moved to the edge of the sofa and took another sip of the water. She placed the bottle on the coffee table and started. She knelt down, picked up a *Glamour* magazine from the side table with one hand and with the other picked up a used tissue like it was a biohazard, and held them both out to Tim.

He looked a bit worried and said, "That's my mother's magazine."

She opened up the door to the end table, smiled and maintained eye contact with him the whole time as she pulled out a hand lotion pump then a box of tissues and placed them on the table. She looked at him expectantly.

"Uh, allergies and dry skin," he said weakly.

She reached back into the cabinet, pulled out a ruler and placed it on the table while wearing a smug grin.

Tim, dying a bit now, said, "Okay, I don't even know what that's doing there."

As she reached to open the table drawer he said, "Wait!" Unsure what to do, he sat on the edge of the sofa, mortified. She paused and smiled, then opened the drawer and pulled out a sheet of paper; an incredibly old, discolored, beaten up sheet of paper. On the top of the page written sloppily were the words 'Growth Chart' and under that was a graph. She stood and took a moment to examine it. He sat back on the sofa, busted, and wiped his sweaty hands on the towel.

Like a lawyer cross-examining a witness who was about to crack, she gave him time to stew. She paced around a bit and alternated between eyeing the page carefully and glancing at him about to speak then back to the page, then finally she looked at him and said, as if she couldn't believe her eyes, "Does this go all the way back to 99?"

He swallowed hard and said barely audibly, "98."

She gave him a look which said, '*I didn't quite get that.*' He looked down to the carpet then to her expression and finally he spilled it, "98. I started that in 98, okay?"

This brought a smile to her face, "And you saved it. That's sweet. In a totally bizarre way." She returned her attention to the sheet and studied it some more. "And you kept measuring all these years. But it looks like there's been no change since like, 2003."

Tim took on a defensive tone. "First, until recently it was only an annual measurement. Second, back in 2005 there was an increase."

She looked a little more intensely at the sheet then a smile hit her face. "Oh, I see it yeah! An eighth of an inch."

"It's closer to three sixteenths," he said smugly.

She gave the sheet a confused look. "It goes off the top of the page here."

He pointed at the sheet as he said, "Uh, fold up the flap."

She struggled with it a little as he pointed again to the top of the page, "It's the flap."

She turned it over, discovered the newly taped-on flap in the upper right of the page and folded it up. Graphed on the flap were the results of the recent huge increase. She narrowed her eyes and was blown away. All she could muster was, "Whoa!"

She looked at him, mesmerized as he leaned back into the sofa and closed his eyes with his head back. Jill moved to the back of the sofa, "Remember how I would relax you with those scalp massages?"

She slid in close to him from behind and gently ran her fingers through his hair, "Your hair is so full now." Then she added soothingly, "Sshhh, it's okay. It's going to be okay."

With one hand she unbuttoned her shirt and pulled it open, exposing her unrestrained gorgeous breasts. She returned both hands to his hair then ran them down to his chest and he exhaled deeply. They were both getting into it. She looked to his groin and there was evidence that her touch was starting to have the desired result. She said sexily, "Remember how hard this used to get you?"

She brought her hands back up to his hair and pushed her breasts even harder into his head. He began rubbing his head slowly all over her heaving chest. She closed her eyes and massaged his head vigorously as he reached full staff now with the towel straining.

As they enjoyed the moment, both with closed eyes, open mouths and heavy breathing, Tim's hair unfortunately began falling out in large clumps; really large clumps. Most of it was all over her breasts. To someone walking into the room, it would have appeared that the hair was actually growing out of her chest and it was a truly freakish scene. Nothing spoils a gorgeous set of tits more than thick dark chest hair sprouting up between them.

Jill felt something wasn't quite right first, and opened her eyes to see Tim's patchy bald head. "Aaahhh!" She freaked out, flicking the hair off her with both hands and it landed all over Tim.

He opened his eyes and looked at the hair, shocked and exclaimed, "What the hell?"

She jumped back and began buttoning her shirt as Tim quickly stood with the hair pouring off his chest and lap onto the floor. The hair that fell out was only the new pill-educed strands from the very top of his head. This left him mostly bald on top, except for a few patches, with the bald area now starkly contrasted by the long hair around it which had recently grown in. He looked sort of like a deranged circus clown, minus the wacky makeup. He turned to her, rubbed the top of his head and the rest of the patches on the very top came off in his hands. As he looked at his hair-covered hands, she eyed his hair while holding back a laugh. Then she looked down to the towel sticking straight out from his unbelievably enormous boner and said, "Oh my God!"

Tim, unaware of his towel condition and still focused on his hair issue, moved a step to catch a glimpse of his head from the mirror on the wall and looked at himself, mortified. "I know. I look like a freak!"

"Not your hair," she said. As he ignored her and continued to pull on his hair and study it in the mirror she added, "I think it's definitely time for a new measurement." Then she paused open-mouthed and added, "I have to see it."

He turned to look at her as she pointed to his groin in awe. He still hadn't looked down yet and he glared at her. "My hair is falling out and God knows what else might be falling OFF and you want to see my dick. What's wrong with you?"

He narrowed his eyes at her and she was still fixated on the towel. He followed her gaze and as he looked down at it, he suddenly became dizzy due, of course, to the huge amount of blood that was being stolen from the rest of his body to support this unnaturally large appendage. He looked back up to her, lightheaded, and his eyes rolled back in his head. He grabbed the wall as she rushed to him and helped him to the sofa.

She ran to the kitchen then returned with a bottle of water and a cool cloth. She opened the bottle and handed it to him. He looked at her thankfully, took a sip then leaned his head back on the sofa. She grabbed the bottle from his hand then placed the cool cloth over his eyes.

She knelt down close to him in genuine concern and began stroking his face gently. She looked back down at the fully tented towel with renewed interest, checked to be sure his eyes were still covered then slid over a little and got between his spread legs without touching him. She carefully grabbed the two corners of the towel and slowly began lifting them up, alternating between watching for Tim's reaction and attempting to catch sight of it.

Tim said, "Wh-What happened?" as he brought his hands to his face to touch the cloth. She sprang up and grabbed his hands and guided then back down on the sofa, "Just rest. You almost fainted." She slid back down and returned to removing the towel. She gingerly lifted it up off his huge erection and her face told the story. Now free from the towel, it sprang up and swelled even larger. The giant thing sort of pulsated, swelling with each beat of his heart. Jill checked to be sure his eyes were still covered, then fixated back on his penis and reached out slowly to touch it. As she reached for it, something made her look at Tim's balls.

Tim's balls were unfortunately the exact same pathetically small size they had been before all the immense penile growth. This completely sidetracked Jill and she could not control her reaction. The smile on her face became a chuckle and finally a full on laugh. The tiny balls were a severe contrast to the Washington Monument sized erection that towered over them. When Tim heard her, he raised his head and the cloth fell from his eyes.

As she continued to laugh, he blinked as he struggled to focus on what she was seeing. When his vision returned, his jaw dropped and he stared at his penis truly horrified, but a little impressed and said, "What the fuck?" He glanced down at her and frowned when he saw that she was laughing. "What the fuck are you laughing at?"

"I'm sorry. I'm sorry. It's nothing," she said as she covered her mouth trying to contain her outburst.

He glared at her, "What the hell could you possibly be making fun of now? It's freaking huge."

She looked at him while biting her lip and shook her head no with a silly look on her face. "Really it's nothing."

"What is it?" he demanded.

She tried to get it out without laughing, but failed miserably and chuckled her way through saying, "It's just your balls. Have you noticed your balls?"

"What the hell is wrong with them?"

"Well, the three piece set kinda doesn't go together anymore, don't you think?" She laughed a little more and then got up and sat next to him on the sofa.

"Okay, so maybe they're a little small, but they are nothing to laugh at," he said, folding his arms and giving her an irritated look.

On the sofa her smirk turned back to a mesmerizing stare as she looked back at his giant penis and said, "But my God you are big. I've seen a lot of porn and I don't..." She panted as if she was trying to catch her breath and whispered, "Let me touch it. I have to."

He looked at her. She was now gazing at him just as a lion would a gazelle seconds before ripping it to pieces. She slowly reached to touch it. He quickly pulled the towel back over it, stood up, scowled at her and said, "Maybe if you hadn't been laughing at my balls I would have let you!"

"Oh come on, they are a little bit--" She cut herself off when she saw the look on his face.

He covered his bald head with one hand and his groin with the other and said, "I think you should go."

She slid closer to him on the edge of the sofa and said, "Just let me touch it for a minute."

"Get out."

He backed away from her and she stood up slowly and looked at him with disappointment.

He repeated, "Get out."

Jill looked down at the towel once more, paused, and still appeared to be in a trance like state when she said, "You know, maybe they make a ball enlargement pill, that will, you know, even everything--"

"GET OUT!" he yelled.

She snapped out of it and gave him a look that told him she had been insulted, then turned to go.

thirty one - Shit, it's bigger. Isn't it? How's that even possible?

At the abandoned house, Larry maintained his surveillance of the white house until he heard a car door slam. He swung his binoculars over and caught Jill speeding down the Garrett driveway. To get Sam's attention he said loudly, "She's leaving already."

As Jill was speeding away, Tim was seated nude at his measuring station with his huge erection still in full glory. He eyed it suspiciously and readied the ruler for a measurement. When the ruler came up way short, his hand began to shake and he attempted to use his finger to mark his penis at twelve inches and then slide the ruler up to that point to complete the measurement. His finger and ruler kept sliding down and he tossed the ruler across the room in frustration. He stood, paused briefly to think and spotted one of his large packing boxes across the room.

Larry scanned the Garrett house with the binoculars and caught sight of Tim standing in a room and was rewarded with a clear view of Tim's massive manhood in the process. Larry said, "Get the hell over here. You've got to see this." He couldn't believe his eyes and he shook his head and tried to refocus, but when he looked back, Tim was gone. Larry said, "I don't know where he went."

Sam rushed over, binoculars in hand and took a look out the window. They both scanned over to another window just in time to get a view of Tim's naked ass as he bent over a box in a desperate search. They both exclaimed with profanity, tore their eyes away from it and frowned at one another.

Larry said slowly and a little sickened, "Wait, you've got to see him when he turns around."

They gave each other a look as if they had smelled something foul and slowly resumed looking out the window. They returned just in time to see Tim pull something from the box and turn to face them. Sam focused in on Tim's head and said, "Shit, what happened to his hair?"

Larry focused on the actual problem area and said, "Never mind the hair, look a little lower."

Sam brought his attention about two feet lower and nearly dropped the binoculars when he saw it. Larry lowered his binoculars away from his face as did Sam and they slowly turned to look at one another, almost in slow motion, and shared a dazed look.

"Shit, it's bigger. Isn't it? How's that even possible?" Sam said as they both returned to spying on Tim, but when they looked where they had last seen him, he was gone.

Larry found him again first and directed Sam back to the right. When they both located him again, Tim was seated on the sofa holding a tape measure and sporting the giant entity of an erection. He extended the tape out two feet and measured his world record boner. Tim's jaw dropped, along with the two spies, as he clocked in at just over sixteen inches. Tim let the tape retract and then he let the measure fall from his hand to the sofa. He slowly reached out and picked up the MaxiManhood pill bottle from the table and studied the label on the back carefully as Sam and Larry lowered their binoculars and shared another dumfounded look.

Sam returned to Tim with the binoculars and noticed he was holding the pills and commented, "He's holding a pill bottle."

Tim alternated between reading it, looking down at himself in a panic, then returning to the bottle. Sam continued, "I can't make it out. It starts with an M. It says Max something." Then Tim stood up and walked out of their view taking the bottle with him. Sam said, "Damn it, he's gone," and he looked at Larry. "I'm not nuts right? It's definitely bigger now, like a whole lot fucking bigger, right?"

Larry just nodded and said, "He needs a freaking tape measure now!"

"No wonder she ran."

Larry thought for a moment, smiled, and said, "That must be one of those penis enlargement pills."

"Those don't actually work, right?"

"Maybe he found the one that does."

They looked at each other a little perplexed until Larry said, "Would you ever take something like that?"

Sam said smugly, "No, don't need it."

"Oh, me neither."

In the bathroom, Tim stood near the counter, utterly terrified as he examined his incredible penis from different angles in the mirror. Amazingly, it had grown more than four inches over his target length and it was so thick he could only get his hand about two thirds of the way around it. He turned his attention to the MaxiManhood pill bottle and read the label once more. He looked back at his penis and all he could say was, "Shit."

As he looked at it, he thought for a second about possibly attempting a career in porn, but then realized he would never be able to perform in front of a crew. He couldn't even jerk off in front of Jill that time she had asked him to. He looked up from his groin at his face in the mirror and frowned at his circus freak hair and realized that this look would probably keep him out of the business, anyway.

He tossed the MaxiManhood bottle in the trash and reached into the medicine cabinet and pulled out the ProHairCal and HydroDragenX bottles and also threw them away. He looked again in the mirror at his hair, sighed, then reached under the sink and pulled out the hair clippers.

thirty two - I'm not gonna show you or any other woman IT ever again!

Tim needed to get drunk and fast, so he headed to the pub and sat at the bar drinking a beer with his new, self-inflicted short haircut. Emily entered with two girlfriends and noticed him. Her friends moved to a table as Emily walked up to him, smiled, and said, "Like your haircut. So, how's your supply?"

Tim didn't even attempt to give her the impression he was happy to see her and said, "I really don't want to have the playful condom conversation again."

"You'd think with what you've got going on you wouldn't be able to wipe the smile off your face. Isn't it like every guy's dream to have a bull market going on in his pants?" she said. At first this only was amusing to her, but she stared at him grinning long enough to break through and eventually Tim cracked a smile.

A few drinks later, Tim was visibly loaded. He sat at a table with Emily and her two friends; the mostly drunk Amy and the mostly sober Helen. Tim said, "I've got to be the only guy on the planet to have a girl break up with him for being too big and for being too small in the same week." He shared a nod with Amy as they each held a shot glass, clinked glasses, and downed them together.

Amy placed her glass on the table and looked at Tim. "That's just awful."

Tim waved his empty shot glass around as he continued, "It's like that story. Goldilocks. First she was like…" Tim switched to a falsetto voice each time he imitated Goldilocks' complaints, "This dick is TOO small. And then she was all like, this dick is TOO big. When am I going to hear ahhh, this dick is just right?"

Amy and Helen looked at each other for a brief second, shared a smile, and then loudly spelled the letters in unison, "S. A. T. C."

Tim and Emily gave them a strange glare then looked at each other. Emily shrugged her shoulders to Tim, clueless, then they both looked back to the girls, perplexed.

Amy paused, rolled her eyes and then said, "Sex and the City, duh. You're Goldi-Cocks! Or the girls involved are…"

Helen chimed in with, "There was this one episode where Samantha had like…" She stopped when she saw Tim and Emily both staring at her like she needed to be locked up.

Tim and Emily widened their eyes at each other then each took a sip of their drinks.

"You just need to find the right girl," Amy said switching gears.

"Maybe there's a girl you already know, who —" Helen began, but stopped when Emily kicked both girls under the table. The girls exchanged evil looks and Tim, in his numb state, missed it all.

Tim put down the shot glass, replaced it with his beer pint, took a sip and said, "The right girl doesn't even exist. I'm never dating again. Ever. I'm done with all that shit."

He swallowed the rest of his beer, then gave them a serious look. "All my life I wished and I really believed that having a big dick would be really cool. Well it's not cool. It sucks."

"This is just like this documentary I saw on HBO about guys and their dicks. They told stories about their relationships with their dicks," Helen chimed in cheerily.

"You should do your own documentary," Amy added as Emily glared at her friends. Tim was into it and nodded as he slid his cell phone over to Amy.

"Here, go ahead film it. I didn't tell you about when I was kidnapped and almost raped," Tim said and he proceeded to demonstrate to Amy how to capture video with his phone.

Amy stood, stumbling a little in the process, and prepared to record Tim. "Let's start with a shot of IT first."

"No way. No freaking way. I'm not gonna show you, or any other woman, IT ever again."

Later at the bar, as Emily was returning from the bathroom, she spotted Tim standing on a table surrounded by a crowd. She was stunned and struggled to make her way back to him.

Amy used Tim's phone to capture every second of the goings on. Things became rowdy and the crowd was screaming, "Take it off! Take it off!" Tim looked over them with his hands in the air, welcoming the attention and glory. When Tim unbuttoned his shorts, the crowd began to clap and the bartender glanced over casually as if this type of thing were an everyday occurrence. The crowd of mostly women seemed to be into it, except for one prudish looking woman sitting at the bar. She was dressed in a business suit with her hair up in a bun that was, evidently, way too tight. She glared at the crowd and then looked to the bartender, who was smiling at the scene.

Tim removed his shorts, threw them into the crowd and stood in only boxer briefs with his prominent bulge displayed for his fans. Emily approached the table and tried to get his attention, but was prevented by the large mob. The women started a slow clap as Tim grabbed the waistband on his boxers and announced, "All my life I've been embarrassed in locker room, with women, but no more." Then he ripped his boxers down and his penis spilled out nearly half way down his leg as a cheer erupted from the onlookers. The prudish woman watched in horror as some other women gasped and the few men in the crowd shook their heads in disbelief.

Tim looked over the room proudly, then raised his hands and basked in the cheers for only a moment before he lost his balance and fell off the table and onto the hard wood floor with a horrible thump. Emily pushed her way through the crowd to him. The prudish woman looked to the smiling bartender and gave him an evil glare. The bartender caught the look and returned a 'lighten-up' wave, at which the prudish woman decide to call the police and headed for the bathroom pulling out her cell phone along the way. When Emily reached Tim, she found him barely moving.

thirty three - Good morning wood

The next morning, back at the Garrett house, Tim slept his big night off on the sofa as Emily sat in a chair reading the newspaper. She looked over at him and did a double take when she saw he was sporting rather impressive morning wood. She had heard of this phenomenon, but had never actually experienced it first hand. But this, it was more like a whole forest than a log. She brought the newspaper up to block the view, but then moved it aside and took one more curious glance. But when Tim began to stir, she quickly hid back behind the paper. Tim moved some more, grunted, then sat up and saw her. Tim's boner did not subside, but he was too out of it to notice.

Emily placed the paper on the table and tried to avoid looking at his groin. She shook her head with a gentle smile and said, "Good wood-ing. I mean morning."

Tim missed the reference to his issue and said groggily, "Hey. What happened last night?" as the memories started racing through his mind.

"Let's see," she started and then quickly looked away from him trying to avoid the show in his pants.

He looked down, saw his condition and quickly grabbed a pillow and held it over his lap, "Did I show someone at the bar my--"

"You showed *everyone* at the bar your... It's all in your documentary," she said as she looked back at him, grinning a little when she saw him clutching the pillow.

He gave her a confused look and she added, "Oh yeah, you started filming last night. My friends helped. It's all on your phone. Helen's bringing it over now."

"Why does she--" Tim began, still trying to wrap his head around it all.

"We left it when we were running from the police."

Tim looked at her even more confused. She glanced once more at the pillow in his lap, smiled and looked away.

As Tim unsuccessfully searched his memory for any run-ins with the law, there was a knock at the door. He made a move to stand and Emily jumped up. "Don't get up. I've got it. Really. Don't."

He gave her an odd look then glanced at his pillow-covered crotch and grinned slightly. She opened the door and motioned for Helen to come in. Helen didn't say a word and returned the motion for Emily to come to her. Emily smiled awkwardly at Tim then stepped onto the porch. Tim listened as the two argued outside. The only thing he heard was Emily say, "No, I haven't. I thought you... At least come in and apologize... Hey…" Then he watched Helen through the window as she rushed to her car.

When Emily reappeared from outside, she closed the door and brought the phone to him. She seemed to have something on her mind and he eyed her confusedly. She looked at the pillow, which was still covering his lap, and tried to see if he was still hiding something there and from the looks of how high the pillow was elevated, she was pretty sure that he was. She grabbed another pillow off the sofa and stood looking down at him, holding the pillow in such a way to block her view of the problem area. She said, "Helen couldn't stay and I've got to run, but a couple of things. First, lay off the pills because enough is really enough, okay? I mean really."

She motioned with her head to his groin and he narrowed his eyes oblivious. After a moment he finally glanced down at his lap then he looked up to her, "Oh, sorry." He looked around a little unsure of what to do and she handed him the second pillow and he added it to the pile. As he pushed the pillow into his lap uncomfortably, he said, "I already stopped. But wait. What was that about the police?"

"Forget that; they never saw you. But, I need to tell you something else. One of my soon to be ex-friends kinda slipped you a tiny bit of E last night."

Tim sobered up a little and stared at her, trying to process this as she continued. "She was just trying to cheer you up. I think she was trying to hook us up really. She's a well-intentioned idiot."

"I can't believe you let her do that," he said and he stared at her open-mouthed.

"I swear I didn't know until after. I was in the bathroom when..." she looked at him genuinely sorry, paused, then said, "I'm so sorry."

Tim looked to his phone, then back to her and asked, "So I was slipped the date rape drug?"

"Technically, E isn't 'the date rape drug,' but it does have some of the same--"

"Did we?" Tim interrupted as he looked at her, confused, while making a semi-rude hand gesture.

"No. God no," she said.

Tim looked away and while he stared out the window he said, "I think you should go."

She opened her mouth, but said nothing. She paused briefly, then turned to go.

thirty four - I'm going to take a poll on... his pole

Later, Tim sat on the sofa reviewing the video on his phone. He watched the first twenty minutes, astonished that he could not recall any of it. Mortified from what he had just seen, he closed his eyes tight and shook his head. When he opened them, the video reached the sequence where he climbed on top of the table. Bracing for the worst, he tilted his head away trying to shield his view as he continued to watch. His mouth opened wide when he reached the part where he screamed over the crowd, "All my life I've been embarrassed in locker room, with women, but no more."

Tim watched in horror as he exposed himself to the crowd; he was forced to look away when the video showed a close up of that thing hanging between his legs. He didn't know what to call it anymore, and it didn't look anything like he remembered. The thing wasn't just bigger; it had completely changed shape. Sure he was small before, but he thought it looked pretty good as far as penises go. It wasn't exactly ugly or anything. Girls had actually told him it was cute once or twice. Cute wasn't exactly how a guy would want it to be described, but there are worse ways to be characterized and it was sure worse now. This new monstrosity was hideous and he tried to put the thought of it out of his mind.

He returned to the video and watched the clapping, rowdy shouting and cheering that erupted when he exposed himself, followed by the shaky video of him falling off the table and out of the frame. The video recording showed a view of the stunned faces in the crowd followed by a view of the ceiling as the horrendous sound of him crashing to the floor blasted through the tiny speaker in his phone. Tim cringed.

At the abandoned house, Sam looked out the window with binoculars and said, "We have another package." He watched as the delivery truck driver walked toward the vacant house with the package and rang the doorbell as a car pulled into Tim's driveway. The truck driver waited, but there was no answer at the house. When he turned, the driver spotted Carter getting out of his car in the Garrett driveway, directly across the street, and he called to him. Carter strolled down to the street to meet the driver, signed for and accepted the package, then headed for the Garrett house, package in hand, as the driver left a notice at the door of the vacant house.

Sam watched this scowling and he said, "Fuck, that idiot is giving super cock's friend the package."

Back at the Garrett house, Tim continued watching the video. The footage was a little shaky and dark for a few seconds until Amy turned the camera on herself and drunkenly announced, "Ladies. We're filming a documentary here and I'm going to take a poll on... his pole." The video cut to scenes of random wild girls being interviewed.

"It's awesome. He should really be in porn," said one.

"Woo hoo! I've never seen anything like it," said another.

Amy's voice could be heard saying, "Em, what do you think?" as the shot panned over to Emily, who appeared on screen, speechless. She glanced back to find that Tim was behind her, laughing it up with a group of girls.

Emily looked at the camera, annoyed, and said, "I think this is stupid. He's not just something to be exploited."

The video continued with a view of Emily as Amy's voice could be heard saying, "Well, that sucks. I'm sure that'll be cut right out of the documentary."

Just then Tim heard a knock at the door. He sighed, then shut off the video. He opened the door. Carter handed him the package and rushed past him as he said, "Here. I've got to piss."

Carter hurried to the bathroom as Tim walked to the great room, still reeling from the video. He sat down and began opening the package, without thinking, as he replayed a few of the more embarrassing moments from his film debut in his head.

When Carter emerged from the bathroom, Tim was sitting on the sofa holding a brick of white powder. Carter looked at him, shocked. Three other bricks and the box sat on the coffee table. Carter said, "What the hell are you doing? That's for your neighbor."

"What neighbor?"

"Is that coke?"

"What neighbor?" Tim repeated with an edge to his voice.

"I don't know. The delivery guy said no one was home."

"You mean that empty house across the street with the foreclosure for sale sign?" Tim said, rolling his eyes.

Carter paused for a second and his eyes lit up. "Wait, I've heard of this. They ship drugs to a vacant house and then a drug dealer picks them up so they can't be traced."

"What?"

"Yeah, I saw it on 60 minutes or something."

Carter walked over, took a brick off the table, sat in a chair and he felt the weight of it as Tim slumped back on the sofa. Carter smiled at him and said, "The street value's got to be over 100K."

Tim frowned at him. "Street value, what the--"

"We should sell it," Carter interrupted him, shaking his head with confidence.

Tim said patronizingly, "You're going to move a couple bricks of cocaine? *You*? And then what do we do when the drug dealer comes looking for it?"

"Then we kill him. The world will be a better place with one less--"

"Yeah, you kill him and I'll just run the body through the wood chipper I have out back. Jesus!"

Carter looked at him smugly, "Well, what do you want to do?"

Tim pulled out his phone and just stared at Carter, disgusted, as he dialed 911.

thirty five - Introducing the newly not so well-endowed and really pissed off about it guy

While Tim dialed, the newly not so well-endowed and really pissed off about it guy, Rick, parked his car on the street between the Garrett house and the vacant house. He knew Tim's parents' house was on this street, but he wasn't sure which house it was. He got out of the car, looked around confused, then walked toward the vacant house.

At the abandoned house, Sam finished a call on his cell. Larry looked out the window with the binoculars and spotted Rick lurking suspiciously near the vacant house as Sam walked over, binoculars in hand and said, "Cockboy just called it in. He opened it. It sounds like we got cocaine. Let's get over there."

Larry continued eying Rick and said, "Wait, I've got something."

Sam looked out with the binoculars and focused on Rick.

Rick was on the vacant house's porch holding the delivery tag. Rick studied the tag, spotted Carter's signature then looked around until he recognized Carter's car across the street and he smiled. He crumpled up the tag, dropped it and headed toward the Garrett house as Sam said, "This must be our guy."

Larry and Sam pulled down the binoculars, looked at each other and Larry said, "Shit yeah. We could be going home early today."

Back in the Garrett house, Carter sat on the edge of the sofa and took a quick experimental sniff of the plastic-wrapped white brick.

Tim suddenly looked worried. "What if the drug guy was watching and saw you come over here with the package? He could be heading--"

"Wait, do you hear that squishy sound?" Carter interrupted.

"What squishy sound?" Tim said confused.

Carter scoffed, "The sound of you being such a pussy. Relax. There's--" Before he could finish, someone banged loudly on the front door. Carter dove onto the floor like a little girl and covered his head. Tim was startled, but controlled himself and slipped quickly to the hallway, concealing his body around the corner.

Rick banged again on the door and yelled, "Get the fuck out here. I'm gonna kill you."

Tim looked down at Carter, disappointed. "Yeah and I'm the pussy?"

Rick banged again on the door. Tim said, "It's just Rick," and turned for a quick glance to the foyer sidelight where he spotted Rick the Dick standing on the porch.

Carter stood and pulled himself together as he met Tim at the entrance of the hall. Tim said, "Don't worry. My parents spent a fortune on this super strong door. I think even the glass is like, bullet proof or something."

They both stood smirking and casually watching Rick as he pounded on the door. Rick peered through the sidelight and could spot two figures in the hall. When he looked closer he was sure one of them was Tim. He banged again and said, "I see you there, pussy boy. Open this fucking door!"

Tim looked at Carter and said casually, "Gee, why is everyone calling me a pussy today?"

Rick pounded again at the door as they continued to ignore him and Carter said, "That is a strong door. " He paused looked at Tim and asked, "Fiberglass?"

Tim replied very matter of fact, "No, I think it's steel."

Carter shook his head and muttered, "Huh."

Rick paused and reached for the knob. When he turned it, the door simply opened. He smiled then pushed it open slowly. As Tim watched the door open and the super-irate Rick come into full view, all he could say was, "Shit."

Rick smiled at them and said, "Hey boys." He took two steps into the foyer and grinned, as Carter and Tim stood there, frozen. Then Rick added, "Tim, you're going to tell me how to fix this."

The officers snuck up on each side of the door and peered in. Tim and Carter made eye contact with the officers who signaled them to be still. Rick walked slowly toward Tim and said, "Tell me or I'll kill you, you little freak."

The officers slipped through the door then Sam pointed his gun to the ceiling as Larry put a huge bone crushing hit on Rick and tackled him to the floor. Tim and Carter looked on grinning. Rick was a pretty big guy and Larry wasn't much of a match for him. Rick cursed and thrashed around as Larry tried unsuccessfully to pull his arms back to handcuff him. As Larry struggled to maintain his hold of Rick, he screamed to Sam for help. Sam pulled out a taser and as Larry jumped off, Sam gave Rick a good blast in the side that left him convulsing and drooling on the floor.

thirty six - Oh, no, you'll be fine

Tim, Sam and Carter watched from the porch as Larry dragged the dazed and handcuffed Rick toward the unmarked police car. Rick said, "Wait. What cocaine? What the fuck are you taking about?"

When they reached the car, Larry looked back to Sam, rolled his eyes and said to Rick, "Okay, so then why are you here threatening to kill everyone, huh?"

Rick looked at Larry, unsure whether to admit his penis had shrunk down to infantile proportions, and stammered, "I'm... well, just... he has--"

Larry said sarcastically, "Okay," as he pushed Rick into the car and slammed the door.

Rick turned to look at Tim and screamed from inside the car, muffled but audible, "Tim, tell them who I am."

Sam gave Tim a strange look and said, "How'd he know your name?"

Tim shrugged and turned away.

Tim and Carter sat on the sofa while the cocaine bricks rested on the coffee table in front of them. Sam stood questioning them and making notes and said, "Okay one more question Mr. Garrett. Are you currently taking any meds or supplements of any kind?"

Tim gave him a surprised look. "Uh, why do you need to know that?"

Sam paused, thinking, then spotted the bricks of cocaine and said, "Sir, did you handle those drugs?"

"I did, is that a prob--"

"Bricks of cocaine give off a sort of osmotically reactory, uh…Have you heard of drug interactions?"

"Uh, yeah."

"Now it's important that you remember everything you could have possibly taken recently. Your life could depend on it."

"Well, I was taking this hair growth thing. And uh, vitamin C and D and…"

Sam gave him an impatient look and said, "Yeah, anything else?"

"I was taking a couple other things, but I stopped."

"This is important."

Tim continued, "And this fat burning pill called Hydro something and…" he added while mumbling and looking away, "Maximanho…"

Sam perked up, "Uh, what was that last thing?"

Tim looked back to Sam as he rubbed his hands together nervously. "So that's all of it."

Sam readied his pen and repeated," That last thing was…"

Tim paused as Sam eyed him expectantly, then finally he said loudly, "It's called MaxiManhood, okay?"

"What is that used for?"

Carter grinned and chimed in, "Gee, doesn't that name say it all? I still can't believe you were taking something called Maxi…Manhood."

Sam repeated, "Seriously, what is it used for?"

"It's just this male enhancement thing."

Sam smiled and nodded as he made a note in his pad and said, "Uh huh. That's the one."

Tim suddenly looked worried and said, "Is that a problem? Should I go to the hospital?"

Sam scoffed, "Oh, no, you'll be fine."

Tim and Carter had a look of alarm on their faces as Sam closed his notebook and looked wide-eyed at them grinning. "Thanks, guys we'll be in touch."

"Wait. Don't you need to know what meds I've been taking? I touched the drugs also," Carter admitted.

"No, I'm sure you're okay," Sam said without even looking at Carter as he slapped his notebook against his hand in an apparent signal that he could not wait to get out of there. "Okay then. You boys enjoy the rest of your day."

Carter and Tim shared an odd look as Sam, lost in thought, turned to go without the drugs.

Tim called after him, "Officer White?"

Sam stopped and turned back toward Tim. "What's that?"

Tim gave Sam a look and when Sam just stood there in confusion, Tim finally said, "The drugs? You might want to…"

Sam shot back a forgetful smile, smacked himself in the head with his notebook and said, "It's been a long surveillance and I just spaced out there for a second." He nodded to Tim, then walked over to the table and collected the cocaine.

As Tim stood at the front door, inside the car Sam and Larry were in a semi-heated discussion while Rick mouthed silent threats to Tim from the back seat. Tim playfully taunted Rick, then quickly stopped when Larry got out of the car and approached him. Larry said, "Mr. Garrett, there's one critical question that we forgot to ask."

"What's that?"

Larry pulled out his notepad as he said, "I noticed that you handled those bricks. It's important that we know of any and all meds or supplements that--"

"Oh, the osmotic drug interaction thing," Tim interrupted, casually nodding, as if he knew all about it.

Larry gave him a strange look then played along and added, "Yeah, that uh--"

"I went over all this already with Officer White," Tim said, confused.

Larry murmured, "He doesn't need it, my ass." Tim gave him an odd look as he heard most of Larry's comment, then Larry continued clearly, "If you wouldn't mind, Officer White has a horrible memory."

"Oh, he wrote it down. I watched him."

"And bad penmanship," Larry added tiredly as he readied his pen.

thirty seven - Bret Favre's 'alleged' penis sexting pictures smash Rick the Dick's record

Back at Police Headquarters, Rick underwent some mild to considerably moderate questioning. Then there was the little matter of a full body cavity search, where nearly every officer on duty at the time was an eyewitness to the discovery of Rick's tiny little problem. The rest of the building watched on closed circuit television while others viewed the video later. The laughter could be heard even outside the building during several of the repeat screenings. Rick never mentioned the cause of his issue to Sam or Larry or to anyone else at the station. And while both Sam and Larry considered sharing their knowledge of the MaxiManhood secret with the under endowed Rick, they decided against it. In fact, neither would ever share it with anyone.

Unfortunately for Rick, the pictures from the search were posted on the Internet a few days later, which was just about the time that Rick was released and all charges were dropped. The pictures of Rick's mini member held the record for the most widely viewed penis on the Internet for almost six months. That record was shattered, however, when the 'alleged' Bret Favre's penis sexting pictures leaked onto the Internet in late 2010.

thirty eight - Muffins and Magnums

With Carter out of his hair, Tim could finally finish watching the video of the previous night's events. He sat on the sofa in the great room holding his phone. Just as he started the video, there was a knock at the door. He sighed loudly and again shut it off. When he opened the door, he discovered Rachael holding a gift basket behind her back. A car was waiting in the driveway with a slightly angry looking man sitting in the driver's seat along with Rachael's kids sitting in the back. The man scowled at Tim while the kids were waving at him. He waved to the kids then said to Rachael, "Hey."

She smiled at him, "Bev told me what you did." Tim looked at her concerned and she appeared to be on the verge of tears, but then she stopped herself and added, "I really don't know what to say, except..."

She continued to stare at him teary eyed. When the tension became unbearable for him, he looked down at his feet ashamed and said sheepishly, "You see, I can explain. She can't be satisfied by your average..."

Rachael gave him a clueless look. "What?"

Tim looked back at her, wide-eyed and relieved. "I'm sorry, what were you saying?"

"I'll never be able to repay you, Tim. Or should I call you Magnum P.I.," she said as she smiled and moved the basket in front of her. "I got my job back and I--"

Tim waved her off, embarrassed as Rachael said, "Bev just had the nicest things to say about you. I always thought she was a mean woman, but she's not."

Tim looked away, getting lost in the flashback momentarily, then returned to her and said, "She can be... nice. And she's got a lot of energy for someone her age."

Rachael gave him a strange look, but to Tim's relief she let the comment go. "And I never properly thanked you for Clare's party. I was such an incredible bitch."

"I should apologize for overdoing it. I definitely acted like an ass that night."

"No. No. Sorry I overreacted with... I know it's not much, but here. I made you some muffins."

She handed him the basket. He smiled and said, "Thanks. You wanna come in?"

She waved to the kids in the car and looked at him apologetically. "I can't."

Tim waved again to the kids and took another look at the angry man in the car, who was still staring him down. Tim gave him half a wave and said, "Is that your ex? He looks like he wants to kill me."

"Yeah, he does," she said casually then they looked at each other and shared a smile. "He's getting it together and we're giving it another try for the kids. I'm still in love with him. I feel like I kind of led you on and..."

Tim shook his head. "No, don't. I hope it works out for you both. Really."

"I got you something else. Look under the muffins. Just don't hold them up," she said as she motioned to the basket. Tim moved aside a muffin to find a box of Magnum condoms and he smiled at her. She returned his smile and continued, "You're going to find someone great, I know it. And you'll need those." She kissed him on the cheek then looked at him and said softly, "You might want to look for someone tall. Maybe with wide hips."

He grinned and said, "I'll remember that," a little self-consciously. She turned and headed for the car and he watched her go.

thirty nine - Shrinkage!

Tim sat at the counter holding the box of condoms, smiling. He put them down, grabbed his phone, touched the rewind button on his screen and then touched play. Back on the screen the video started, Emily looked at the camera, annoyed, and said, "I think this is stupid. He's not just something to be exploited."

The video continued with a view of Emily as Amy's voice could be heard saying, "Well, that sucks. I'm sure that'll be cut right out of the documentary."

Emily motioned to cut the video and the shot dropped to an odd angle, but kept rolling. Emily looked away at Tim then back to Amy and in view of the camera said, "I wish I had a chance to date him before. I'm pretty sure he used to be just right." The camera stayed on Emily for a beat then went black. The video continued to several smash cuts of scenes in the bar, back to black, then back to Emily arguing with Helen.

Emily said, "I don't need any help, especially that kind of help. I can't believe you did that to him." Behind Emily the front door could be seen as a police officer entered the bar.

Amy said, "Police. Cool, this'll be awesome for the documentary."

Emily turned along with the camera to witness the prudish woman rush to the officer and point him their way.

Emily could be heard saying, "Oh, shit." The video proceeded with jumpy shots that followed Emily as she rushed over to Tim, pulled him away from some girls and pushed him down, hiding him in a booth. Emily then sprinted to the cop. She hysterically recounted some sort of story to him, collapsed on him in mock terror then pointed to the bathroom. Emily watched the cop get lost in the crowd heading to the bathroom, then she grabbed the confused Tim and dragged him quickly out of the bar.

Amy turned the camera on herself and said, "Tell me you got that."

Tim sat in silence, moved by Emily's performance on the video. He squirmed in the chair a little, then he reached down and uncomfortably adjusted his overabundant package. As he felt his groin, his eyes-widened, he exhaled deeply, pulled his hands up and ran them over his scalp and looked away. Then a thought hit him.

Tim opened up the cover on his laptop computer and typed, "How do I make my penis smaller?" into the Google search bar, and pressed enter. On screen in red appeared: *"Did you mean: How do I make my penis LARGER - Results 1-2 of about 86,232,329."* Below that two ridiculous enlargement results appeared, something about gaining 3 inches in 4 weeks, and another about making her scream. Tim looked down to the bottom of the screen, which showed: *"Click here for results 1 of 1 for "'How do I make my penis smaller?'"*

Tim clicked the link, the screen cleared, then on screen appeared: *"Results 1 of 1 - drshrinkage.com - Proven methods to reduce the size of your penis."*

Drshrinkage.com was a website chock full of helpful hints about making your penis smaller. In fact, it was the only site of its kind created by a doctor with a unique problem – he had a really, really, really big penis. I mean, it was so big that the women he dated wouldn't know what to do with it and he never had sex of any kind; not oral, not vaginal and definitely not the 'other' kind. Well, maybe he got an occasional two-handed handjob, which resulted in intense hand cramping for the giver, but that was about it. Of course this left him incredibly frustrated and he felt that he could never find happiness until he corrected his issue. So after years of research and experimentation, he developed this unique program which somehow actually worked. When he discovered that he wasn't alone and that other men were also plagued with this same affliction, he decided to share his knowledge with the world and thus drshrinkage.com was born.

Tim studied the website closely. He jotted down notes on a legal pad. He printed a number of pages of instructions and recipes from the site and retrieved them from the printer and then it was on.

DAY 1:

In the kitchen, Tim pulled items from a shopping bag and lined them up on the counter including strange-looking roots, mortar and pestle (used to crush things into powder), herbs, lotions, fruits and vegetables, a bag of petite frozen peas and a box of regular-sized condoms.

On the bathroom counter, Tim lined up a tape measure, a standard 12-inch ruler and a 6-inch child's personalized ruler (with "TIMMY" in big white letters along with sports stickers) that Tim had been the proud owner of since he was four years old. He placed all the measuring devices into the medicine cabinet. He taped a computer printed graph titled 'SHRINKAGE CHART' on the wall. The page had 0-20 inches along the side, day 1-7 along the bottom. Day 1 already was marked at 16.5 inches.

Back in the kitchen, Tim pulled the bag of peas from the freezer. He wore a t-shirt and absolutely nothing else, and gingerly placed the bag over his giant flaccid penis. He flinched from the super cold then steadied himself by holding onto the counter. He exhaled, then proceeded to secure the bag around his waist with medical tape.

He leaned over a cutting board of chopped vegetables and fruits as he reviewed a printed recipe. He dropped the sliced items into a blender, half-full of some unidentifiable liquid, then he dumped in a can of some awful jellied brown substance. He looked back to the printed recipe then headed to the pantry.

He returned to the blender with bottles of vinegar and molasses, then carefully measured and poured in the desired amounts and fired up the blender. After the blending, he poured the concoction into a large glass and nearly filled it to the top. He lifted the glass of the chunky brown liquid to his nose, smelled it, retched, then began to drink. He stopped halfway and struggled to keep it down. When he finished, he felt ill.

Tim crushed an assortment of exotic roots and a very small amount of a mild chili pepper into a powder, using the mortar and pestle, as he reviewed the printed documents. He followed the instructions carefully. In a bowl, he mixed various lotions and oils with the powder to create a paste.

He sat up in bed and applied the paste to his entire penis, just as the website had instructed, and while it felt a little cool and strangely tingly, it was certainly refreshing. He pulled up his boxer shorts and smiled confidently. The time was 12:31 AM and he turned off the light and quickly fell asleep.

At 1:15 AM, Tim bolted upright and grabbed his groin in pain. He ripped down his boxer shorts to inspect the area. His penis didn't look inflamed or discolored or anything, but it sure was throbbing in pain. He rushed from bed into the bathroom and took a shower where he washed his groin furiously. When the pain subsided, he returned to bed and went back to sleep.

DAY 2:

Tim awoke with his customary morning wood. He looked at it while still in bed and it didn't look any smaller; in fact it appeared that it might actually be larger. He frowned, rushed to the bathroom and grabbed the tape measure. The measurement came in at a jaw-dropping 18 inches. Frustrated, he tossed the tape measure into the sink then leaned with his erect penis resting on the counter to the chart posted on the wall and marked day 2 at 18 inches and connected the dots.

When he turned back away from the chart, his manhood turned with him, inadvertently sweeping the entire contents of personal care items from the top of counter onto the floor. Tim looked to the sky then down to his mutant self then to the mess on the floor and exhaled deeply. As he angrily retrieved the items, he thought, "How the hell is it actually getting bigger?"

Tim went to the computer and returned to the drshrinkage.com site. He clicked on the FAQ page and scanned the screen. He located the question, "My penis got larger after the first day of treatment. Is this normal?" Tim clicked for the answer and read, "Yes, this treatment may initially cause some unwanted growth. After this period, the trend will reverse and the actual shrinkage process will begin." This satisfied Tim and he gave a matter-of-fact nod.

In the kitchen, Tim drank a full glass of the chunky brown concoction without stopping while again wearing the bag of frozen peas taped to his groin. He retched only once this time, then steadied himself.

Tim sat up in bed and applied the paste to his penis a little more carefully than he did the night before. He was a little scared when he turned off the light at 11:51 PM.

The clock showed 2:16 AM this time when Tim bolted upright in agony, but something now was different with it. The pain was deeper and more intense and it felt like his dick was literally on fire. He rushed into the shower, pulled the showerhead down and directed cold water to the problem area while he grimaced in agony. As he bent with his face smashed onto the tile wall and the water spraying onto his groin, he felt like he wanted to die from the excruciating pain. But the cold water seemed to melt away the pain quickly and he emerged from the shower, too exhausted to do anything but dry off and crawl back to bed.

DAY 3:

Tim awoke again with his normal raging hard-on and hesitantly took a peek at it under the covers. He smiled when he saw that the regiment was finally showing signs of actual shrinkage.

In the bathroom, the measurement came back at just over 14 inches. He marked it on the chart and connected the dots. He was finally heading in the right direction. After another battle to drink down the awful brown concoction, he proceeded with the next stage of the shrinkage plan, which was called extreme ice therapy.

After a quick trip to the store, Tim returned with three twenty-pound bags of ice. He half-filled the bathtub with cold water and dumped in the ice. Tim removed all his clothes, put his hand on the wall for support and gingerly tested the water with his foot; it was fucking cold. Tim pulled his foot back quickly and took a deep breath. He paused, then decided he had to do it. He put one foot into the tub and then the other and stood there shivering, trying to erase the pain from his mind. He squatted down, put his hands on each side of the tub and slowly lowered his body into the icy water until he was sitting in the tub. He shivered as he leaned backward until he was resting his back against the tub. He folded his arms over his chest and sat uncomfortably for the required ten minutes. When he emerged from the tub, he was a strange shade of blue all over and his balls had shriveled up to the size of grapes as they tried to escape the cold.

Then there was another night of pasting his junk and falling asleep dreading the impending, nearly unbearable pain. On this third night he lasted just over four hours and the pain wasn't quite as horrible as in nights past. He again had to rush to the shower and wash off that crap, but the treatment appeared to be working.

DAY 4:

He awoke without wood for the first time in a long time, and he had to work himself up for the daily measurement. After he felt fairly rigid, he looked down on it and was sure that the tape measure was no longer required. He had graduated back to a standard twelve-inch ruler. He clocked in at a healthy eleven and one quarter inch and marked his progress on his chart. His goal was to get back into a regular-sized condom, not the big ones and not the minis, but a good old fashioned regular-sized one. He wanted to fill it out though, and not just have it barely fit, so his plan was to stop the shrinkage therapy exactly when he made it there. Today would be the first condom test day and although his penis was still pretty freaking thick, he decided to proceed with the test.

The test turned out to be a disaster as he struggled mightily trying to put on the condom. It ripped and he examined it, disgusted.

In the kitchen, he drank a full glass of the chunky brown concoction without stopping and almost enjoyed it. He followed that up with another ten-minute hypothermia death bath. That night he applied the paste and wasn't nearly as scared as he had been previously. He slept soundly until morning without any early morning emergency shower required.

DAY 5:

The measurement on this day was eight and three quarter inches and the girth was a little thinner, so Tim's hopes for the condom test were looking up. He struggled putting on the condom, but succeeded. Boy was it tight, though. He smiled at it hesitantly, then felt an odd sensation just before it exploded off his dick, flew up and stuck to the side of his face. He looked at himself in the mirror, with the condom hanging off his face, and had to laugh. He peeled it off and tossed it into the trash, disappointed.

Tim read the newspaper while he dipped toast into a glass of the chunky brown concoction, which he had now developed a real taste for.

After another ice bath he went to sleep with the paste covering his penis for what he felt had to be the last night.

DAY 6:

Tim awoke ready for a measurement. He sat up in bed, removed the covers, pulled his boxers down and took a look at his penis. He remembered the old him and this was pretty close. Maybe slightly longer and thicker, but that would do just fine. He strolled into the bathroom for the official measurement, went into the medicine cabinet for the ruler and then he saw it and he thought, "Yes, I think I'm ready." He pulled the 6-inch 'Timmy' ruler out of the cabinet and looked at it proudly. The ruler was a present that his mother had bought him when he was only a boy. He had colored in the sports stickers on it when he had first received it and he'd used it for measuring things ever since. He switched to using it solely to measure his penis when he was around fourteen. He kept it in the secret hiding place in his closet along with his porno magazine and his penis growth chart. Sadly, he had never outgrown it, well until recently anyway. When he graduated to the standard ruler and then to the tape measure, he thought he would never ever have to go back to old 'Timmy,' but here he was, back again and actually glad to be there.

He placed the ruler next to his manhood (or boyhood, he supposed he could call it now again), and it was a perfect six inches. About half an inch longer than it used to be, and it was definitely thicker than the old Tim, but not freak-show-ishly so.

Now it was time for the big condom test. If he passed it, he would be free of the ice therapy and the awful penis paste, and the chore of having to prepare the brown concoction. He opened the wrapper and tossed it aside.

He placed it over the tip and gently rolled it down. The condom fit well and he knew no explosion was coming up, so he just stared at if for a moment then he pumped his fists in victory facing away from the door.

Unfortunately for Tim and for his father both, this was the moment that Ted Garrett had returned home and entered the bathroom. Ted stood there for a second looking at his son's ass, as he attempted to process the wild scene.

Ted Garrett watched wide-eyed as his naked son danced facing away from him with his fists in the air. When Tim turned to face him, Ted could see that his son was not only hard, but was also for some reason wearing a condom with no female in the general area. There was immense shock on both their faces. And for Tim, there would be a lot of explaining to do, which would include, but not be limited to, the breaking into his old room, the dismantling of the 'sex den,' the driving of the forbidden BMW, and most importantly the defiling of the Theodore Garrett signature dildo, which somehow had disappeared during Tim's stay. As Ted would tell him, those replicas are a real pain in the ass to make.

But that would all come later. Ted gave Tim an odd look, shook his head in mild disbelief, snuck one last quick peek at his son's penis, which they both knew was larger than his own. Tim thought he saw a glimmer of pride shine in his father's eyes. After all, Tim imagined, as a parent, you must want your kids to have more than you had - more money, more success, a better life and yes, even a bigger dick.

Ted simply said, "Good to see you son," and walked out of the room.

forty - I'm going to need to actually see it to confirm that

Days later, after Tim had fully rebuilt the sex room and was allowed to leave the house again, he traveled to the drug superstore to find Emily. She wasn't working a register or the customer service desk that day, but he recognized her car in the parking lot. He ended up asking an associate where she was and was directed to the back of the store.

He found her restocking pads in the Women's Heath/condom aisle. When he approached they made eye contact, but neither of them spoke. Instead, he grinned, then casually walked past her to the condom section and she played along. He said, "Excuse me, miss."

"Yes, sir?" She strolled over, all business. "How can I help you?"

"I need some condoms."

She looked him over from head to toe. "Would you say you're average, above average, below average, or what?"

"Originally below, then I was above, but now I think I've leveled off."

They each picked up a box of condoms and pretended to study them. Emily said, "That's odd. Sounds like you need a personalized condom fitting."

"I didn't know you did that here."

"Yeah, the old pharmacist does. He's an ex-marine. Does it right there in the back."

"I think I met him. He doesn't like me."

"He doesn't like anyone."

Tim laughed, then tried to put on a sober face as he said, "Okay, enough with the condom jokes. Seriously, can we..." He stopped when he saw that she was still smiling at him and he frowned. She attempted to pull herself together and was having a difficult time, but he continued anyway. "I watched the video. That was something, how you saved me from the police that night."

"That was all on there, huh," she said, looking at him. "It was the least I could do after my friend drugged you."

"Did you mean all that stuff about wishing you had a chance to date me before...And all that just right stuff you said?"

She nodded and looked at him, a little embarrassed.

Tim looked deeply into her eyes. "Because I think I'm more or less just right again."

"I'm going to need to actually see it to confirm that," she said as she smiled and moved a little closer to him. "But you said you're not showing it to women anymore. Or dating again."

He narrowed his eyes and said, "I never... Okay, maybe I said that." He moved in close to her for a kiss. "But I'm willing to make an exception."

They kissed and it was long and passionate. At about the same time, they both realized they were still holding the condom boxes. They broke the kiss, glanced at the boxes then gave each other a look. Then they dropped the boxes to the floor and got back to it...

epilogue(s) - Have anything bigger?

RICK THE DICK:

Rick sat on an examining table in a doctor's office wearing only a gown that opened in the front. For such a big strong guy, the doctor had never seen such a small penis. The doctor sat in a chair in front of Rick and held some sort of magnifying lens to look closely at his shrunken, baby-sized genitalia. The doctor rolled his chair back away from Rick while scratching his head, then looked back to him once more and exhaled deeply. He paused and all he could think to say was an unconvincing, "Huh."

The doctor rested his elbows on the arms of the chair, and used his index fingers to hold up his chin. "I've never seen a better candidate for penile lengthening and thickening surgery. Let me walk you through it."

The doctor rolled his chair over to a desk, picked up a detailed 3-D model of the male reproductive system, then rolled back to Rick. "First, we sever the suspensory ligament that attaches the penis to the pubic bone." The doctor struggled to pull the detachable penis from the model. When it finally came off, it slipped from his hand and crashed to the floor. Rick stared at him, unfazed. The doctor smiled at Rick and quipped, "Don't want to do that in the O.R." Rick ignored the joke.

After picking up the fallen penis from the floor, the doctor mounted it higher on the model. "Then we move and reattach it to create a longer penis."

Rick leaned forward wide-eyed and said, "Okay. Okay."

The doctor continued, "Then we make the penis thicker by suctioning fat from a fleshy part of the body and injecting that fat into the penis."

Rick gave him an optimistic look and said, "Let's do it. When can you schedule me in?"

JILL THE SIZE QUEEN:

Jill stood at the counter of an adult novelty store. The clerk handed her a giant mutant dildo, like the biggest freaking one in the world. She studied it carefully, looked at it from all angles, then frowned. She shook her head and asked, "Have anything bigger?"

THE BASKETBALL GUY WHO "DIDN'T NEED IT":

That day when Tim revealed the new him, this guy was the first to say he didn't need it. Well, he acted like he needed it all right. While Tim and all the other guys were showering, he snuck to Tim's locker, retrieved the phone number printed on the bottle of magic pills and placed an order minutes later.

After taking them for four weeks there had been absolutely no change whatsoever. He called

MaxiManhood Laboratories to take advantage of the money back guarantee and was told a credit would be processed against his card. A week later there was still no credit. Instead, a second bottle arrived along with a second charge. Even after multiple phone calls, each ending with a promise to "fix" the problem, the monthly deliveries continued and so did the charges until he finally cancelled his credit card. Currently, his complaint against the company is pending, along with dozens of others, with the attorney generals office.

THE DEDICATED POLICE OFFICERS:

Officer Sam and Officer Larry opened up their respective doors in their respective houses at just about the same time to find a package on their respective porches. They each picked them up and checked the sender name. Both packages read MaxiManhood Laboratories.

They each smiled, looked both ways to check for anyone watching, then carried the packages inside and closed the doors.

TIM AND EMILY:

On exactly date number three, and no the night at the bar did not count, the couple planned to do it. While the two previous real dates were amazing and this couple was clearly clicking, there was absolutely no nudity involved in either date. Sure there was some intense making out and pawing as they groped each other for thirty minutes when he dropped her off at her apartment, but they both decided to take it at least semi-slow.

Emily wanted Tim so badly that for the first time ever, after both dates, she found herself masturbating before Tim's car even left the parking lot. Emily left him so worked up that he was forced to relieve the uncomfortable pressure he was feeling on the drive home, which he found a little tricky, but still manageable. Emily had yet to see the incredible transforming penis and her curiosity was piqued.

On the big night there would be no lobster, but Tim did prepare her a mostly edible meal. Emily bought something special to wear and while Tim waited in her bed she put it on in the closet in order to surprise him. She didn't know that he had also planned a surprise.

When Emily emerged from the closet wearing a fiery red teddy, she found Tim under the covers with a nearly two-foot tent at his groin. His jaw dropped when he saw her and he forgot briefly about the joke. She stopped in her tracks, eyeing the enormous bulge as he continued to stare at her, nearly drooling.

She said, "Tim, what is that? I thought you--"

"What?" Tim replied still dazed.

Emily walked over to him slowly and mostly horrified while pointing to his groin and added, "Did it go back?"

Tim finally snapped out of it, looked at her face instead of her gorgeous tits, which were pretty clearly visible through the lace teddy, and said, "Oh this. Sorry I was just playing a little joke." He proceeded to fish out the curling iron tent pole from under the covers.

She smiled at him, took the iron from his hand and placed it on the bed. "All right. Now I've got to see it."

"Knock yourself out," he said with a grin.

She pulled the covers off him and he was nude and totally ready to go. She looked at his penis and smiled, "Oh it's nice and, I don't normally swear, but it's pretty fucking big I'd say."

"Seriously?"

"Yeah," she said genuinely as she climbed on top, straddling him. She looked down at it again and added, "Is this the size it was before all the... experimentation?"

"Yes, exactly the same. I have the documentation to prove it."

She narrowed her eyes and looked at his face. "Then what was the big deal? Why'd you try to change?"

He paused. "I really don't know."

They shared a smile, he kissed her and it was on. Twenty-three minutes later, thanks to some obscure sex angling technique he read about, Tim gave Emily a fully hands-free orgasm.

CARTER:

Carter wore only boxer shorts as he sat on the sofa with his chest, biceps and abs connected to the AutoXerSizer. The two remaining AutoXerSizer pads were dangling unconnected on the floor.

Carter was particularly captivated with Kelly and they had been seeing each other, sort of, since Carter had rescued her from the closet.

Kelly just happened to be in his apartment on this day and Carter looked hesitantly at the last two unconnected AutoXerSizer pads. She stood next to him wearing a leather bra and panty set and holding a small whip. She didn't appear all that happy. He hated it when she was unhappy. As in he really, really hated it.

She nodded with a determined look then struck the sofa near him moderately hard with the whip. He smiled at her; a mostly Stockholm Syndrome'ish smile, and then he connected the final two pads inside his underwear right to either side of his manhood.

She opened each of the three pill bottles, the same magic combination that had proven so successful for Tim, and handed them to her willing boy toy. He was well aware of the effect that this procedure had on Tim and Carter made no attempt to swallow the pills. He just stared at her.

She looked back at him, rolled her eyes, then grasped the front clasp in her bra and released it. The bra fell to the floor and her beautiful full breasts bounced slightly and stared right back at him. His jaw dropped and he tossed the pills inside his mouth. She straddled him on the sofa and put the water bottle to his mouth. He took a sip, quickly swallowed the pills and leaned his head on her breast. She pushed a nipple into his mouth, let him nurse for only a moment, then she pulled away and said, "Ready?"

She didn't wait for an answer, jumped off him and proceeded to turn on the device, rolling the dial up to the 5 setting. A soft humming emanated from the machine and she watched Carter as his body started to gently shake. She smiled then turned the dial to 10. The humming grew louder as Carter's body trembled. The unit began to smoke and his head started shaking violently.

The humming increased even louder as the lights dimmed in the room. A loud pop was followed by a last spasm through Carter and...

THE END

author's note - My Apologies to Mr. Costner and a note about Bret

I didn't mean to throw Kevin under the bus back in chapter one. I really didn't. I was just trying to make a point. I'm a big fan of his work. I love *Tin Cup* and I kind of lose it at the end of *Field of Dreams* every time I watch. That might say more about the poor relationship that I have with my father than anything else, but still it is a great film.

Sorry, back to Kevin. I'm sure Mr. Costner is more than adequate down there; chicks really seem to dig him and it can't only be because he's super rich, can it? Anyway, if that really did happen (as it was reported) at the test screenings of *For Love of the Game,* then it's just more proof that groups of people can really act like complete assholes sometimes. Kevin doesn't deserve that kind of shit.

And a few words about Bret. The Kevin Costner situation might not have been the perfect teachable moment for Bret, but let this be one of those moments for all men, especially famous ones. Unless your penis is huge, it's only going to be made fun of if you make it public. You should be able to look down and make that determination; it really isn't that difficult. Plus, it seemed to everyone else on the planet, except maybe Bret, that the target of his affection had no interest in him whatsoever.

She didn't seem to be on the fence, not even close, and even if she was, sexting pictures of that particular penis was really not going to push her over to the other side. Bret can certainly throw a pass a lot longer than most guys, but unless something else is a lot longer it's not a real good idea to put it on display. Way to go Bret, allegedly.

Oh, and I know what you're thinking. The answer is no there will not be a 'shrinkage 2, the RISE of Carter' sequel.

acknowledgements

If it hadn't been for Jackie Winebrenner, I never would have finished this novel. She encouraged my writing more than anyone on the planet and I probably never would have finished had it not been for her.

I'd also like to thank my editor, Jackie Ernst, for polishing the hell out of this thing, improving my writing tremendously and pulling me back where needed and making this story what it is today.

I'm grateful to those who submitted themselves to early versions of this story, including Matt Zettell, M. Toomey and David Lammey. Your story suggestions and support were invaluable in this process.

And thank you to Laurie Hardjowirogo for coming up for the concept that eventually became the cover design and for a tremendous amount of advice along the way which helped make this book a reality.

CPSIA information can be obtained at www.ICGtesting.com
Printed in the USA
BVOW00s1049301013

335002BV00003B/46/P

9 780692 012031